MIDDLEBURY SANITARIUM

Moving In Series Book 3

RON RIPLEY

ISBN: 979-8-89476-013-1
Copyright © 2016 by ScareStreet.com

This is a work of fiction. Any resemblance to actual persons, living or dead, or actual events is purely coincidental.

Enter the Realm of Terror...

We'd like to take a moment to thank you for your support and invite you to join our VIP newsletter.

Dive deeper into the darkness with exclusive offers, early access to new releases, and bone-chilling deals when you sign up at www.ScareStreet.com.

Let the nightmares begin...

See you in the shadows,
Scare Street

CHAPTER 1

MIDDLEBURY SANITARIUM

The King waited patiently.

He had learned the difficult practice over decades.

Now he stood on the widow's walk of the house and looked down upon his domain. He could see the small light in the guardhouse glowing. The old man would be there, the King knew, with a pipe in his mouth and a book in his hand.

Yet the old man was a good watchman. He patrolled the King's land and protected his houses. He was perhaps gentler than the King would prefer, but the guard was a man who maintained the peace.

A loud creak followed by a thump, shattered the silence of the King's quarters.

He turned away from the window and made his way down a flight of stairs to the main hall. He paused and listened.

Footsteps on the floor.

The King retreated into his study and went to stand by the fireplace. He rested a hand on the marble mantle but kept his eyes on the doorway.

A red light played across the hallway's parquet floor, and the King heard voices.

"...don't have to worry," a man said.

"Why don't we have to worry, Ben?" another man snapped. "You didn't tell me there was going to be a guard! Christ, if we get caught, I'll lose my chance at making partner!"

"Calm down, Chad," Ben replied. "You know, for a big brother you're a pansy sometimes."

"Shut up, you're not the one risking anything."

Ben laughed. "Yeah, I am. Another trespassing charge and I go away for a while. And not to Valley Street Jail, either. The men's prison in Concord.

World of difference from what I hear."

Chad sighed, and the two men appeared in the doorway.

They stopped, and the King examined them. Tall young men clad in identical clothing of all black. They had even rubbed some sort of coloring onto their faces, for while they had the rich coloring of Africans, they had none of the features one could attribute to Americans of the race. Nor did they enjoy the fine, beautiful facial structures of the Masai or the Zulu.

Common crooks, the King decided.

"Look at this detail work," said Ben.

"Wow," Chad said in a low voice. "Will it be safe to take pictures in here?"

"Of course," Ben said, slipping his phone from a pocket.

"What about the security guard?"

"Chad, did you see him? The guy's got to be at least seventy. Besides, when I scoped the place out last night the majority of the time he's in there puffing away at a pipe and reading."

"What if he walks around?" Chad said nervously. "I mean, what if he does some sort of patrol?"

"Gimpy as hell I bet," Ben answered with a chuckle as he put his flashlight away. "Anyway, my scaredy cat big brother, let's get some pictures."

"Don't call me a scaredy cat," Chad grumbled, shutting off his own light. "I don't like it."

"I know," Ben laughed. "Why do you think I do it?"

"You're a pain."

"Yup."

They were taking pictures of his house.

Anger boiled up within him, and the King stepped away from the hearth.

Chad paused and lowered his camera. "Did you hear anything?"

"No," Ben replied as he took a picture of the tin ceiling. "What do you think you heard?"

"A footstep."

"Naw," Ben replied, moving to take a picture of the wainscoting. "I didn't hear anything, Bro."

The King made his way between them.

Ben lowered his camera. "I felt something, though."

"Cold?" Chad asked.

"Yeah," Ben started, but the King interrupted him when he slammed the door closed.

"Jesus!" Chad yelled, spinning around.

"Oh my God," Ben whispered.

The King took a step towards them.

"What?" Chad asked, turning to look at his brother.

"I snapped a picture just as the door was closing. Look."

Ben held his camera out to Chad.

"Oh Sweet Mary Mother of God," Chad said, crossing himself. "Is it a person?"

"I think so," Ben said.

The King moved closer.

"It's cold in here," Chad said.

"We need to leave," Ben said. "We need to leave now, Chad."

"Okay," Chad said. "Alright."

Ben tried to open the door, but it wouldn't budge.

"Come on, Ben," Chad said nervously, "let's go."

"I'm *trying*."

"Try harder!"

"It is no use," the King said. "I do not wish you to leave."

And the King unleashed his wrath.

CHAPTER 2:
A JOB PROPOSITION

Brian sat in the waiting room of Kerouac Realty and fidgeted with the rings on his index fingers. He sat in a leather chair and fought the desire to fall asleep. He was tired from a long night of research, and the exquisite comfort of the seat was not helping him stay focused.

He stifled a yawn and straightened up. Soft music drifted down from hidden speakers promising sweet dreams and relaxation.

The young woman behind the front desk looked up at him and smiled. A large, dark wooden door to the left of her desk opened and a man in his late forties waved at Brian.

"Mr. Roy," the man said. "I'm Joe Kerouac. Come in, please."

Brian stood up, nodded to the receptionist and walked into the office. He took a seat in a short, dark blue club chair as the real estate agent closed the door behind him.

"Coffee, Mr. Roy?" he asked, pausing by a long sideboard to pour himself a cup.

"No thank you," Brian said. "And you can call me Brian."

"Well, a pleasure, Brian," he said as he sat down at his desk. He reached over and offered his hand, which Brian shook. "You can call me Joe. I appreciate you coming to see me. It's not often I have to call someone into my office like this."

Brian nodded. "So, Joe, tell me what it is you need the Leonidas Group for. This is just as different for me. Usually, I have a homeowner, or a tenant call us. Occasionally we'll get a landlord. This is a first, though."

"Good," Joe smiled. "We're both starting from the same place, then."

Brian chuckled. "I guess we are. Alright, tell me what's going on."

"It's fairly straightforward," Joe said, leaning back in his chair. "I represent a client who is interested in purchasing the old Middlebury

Sanitarium. Do you know anything about the facility?"

"No," Brian said, shaking his head. "I can't say I do."

"Fair enough. Middlebury Sanitarium is located right outside of Stark, New Hampshire. It is a large campus, seven main buildings, a dozen smaller residences, and tunnels connecting them all. It's located on roughly four hundred acres of land, and it's pretty damned isolated. Originally it was a tuberculosis ward, then afterward, it served as a mental health facility and poor house up until the late nineties. For the past twenty years, it's been empty. Not abandoned, mind you, just empty. All of the buildings were winterized, and there is a security firm which patrols the property."

"So we've got a big old place up in the middle of nowhere?" Brian grinned.

Joe smiled. "Exactly right, Brian. Exactly right. Now my client is interested in the property. They haven't told me why, and I don't really care. I like my commission, and if this goes through, I'll be just about set to retire. That being said, my client is a little, well, they're a little strange."

"How so?" Brian asked.

"They're concerned the property might be haunted."

"And if the sanitarium happens to have a few residential spooks?"

"The deal may well be off the table," Joe said with a sigh. "Now normally I would slip you a couple of hundred and a wink and get some hustler to say it's not haunted. In this instance, my client could well ruin my life if I tried to brush anything under the table."

"At least you're honest about it," Brian said.

"When I have to be," Joe said. "Anyway. My client has authorized me to pay you whatever you want for a thorough investigation of the property. And what they mean by thorough, is finding out first if there are any ghosts. Second. If there are, how many? Third. Why are they there? And finally, how to get rid of them. My client is motivated. They want the property. But they are not going to move forward on the deal if there are 'ghosts' there."

Joe leaned forward and smiled. "So, Brian, there's my basic question. Can you get rid of ghosts?"

"I can tell if the sanitarium is haunted and whether or not spirits can be convinced to move on. I cannot promise you I can help them pack bags and get on down the road."

Joe grinned. "Fair enough, Brian. Tell me what you need for a retainer and we'll get this ball rolling."

CHAPTER 3

KEN BUCKINGHAM ON THE GRAVEYARD SHIFT

Ken sat in his chair in the guardhouse at the gate to the Middlebury Sanitarium.

The chair had been his since 1969.

Officially he had retired in 2010, but he was still doing the same job. Nothing had changed, and Ken was perfectly fine with that.

He opened the top right drawer of his desk and took out his tin of pipe tobacco and his pipe. The clock in front of him clicked from eleven o'clock to one-minute past. A barn owl that had taken up residence in the main building's bell tower went screeching past.

Ken raised his pipe to the bird, murmuring, "Good hunting."

He started to pack sweet, cherry tobacco into the four-inch deep wooden bowl of his pipe. The pipe would last him two hours, give or take a few minutes.

Bits of tobacco leaves stuck beneath his thumbnail and stained the calluses on his fingers. Soon he had a pleasant cloud of smoke above his head.

But his back ached, and his knees complained. The old scars on his head itched and his right ear felt smothered.

Everything was normal.

Ken clamped down on the pipe stem before he pulled on his black watchman's cap and then his gloves. He double checked the buttons and the Velcro flap on his long jacket. His flashlight hung from his belt, the tool powerful enough to light up the face of a building, and warn any trespassers Ken was on his way through.

He let out a long stream of smoke, adjusted his glasses, and opened the door. The cold, January air slapped at his exposed face. He liked the brutal chill of the New England winter. It served to remind him how lucky he was to have made it back from the humid heat of Vietnamese jungles.

Ken locked up the office behind him and started his patrol.

The grounds of the Middlebury Sanitarium were lit only by starlight and the half-moon. His own little guardhouse was powered by a set of solar panels and a battery. It was only enough power for his small heater and a light he used for reading.

The jangle of the keys was slightly muffled as he walked, trapped between his jacket and his hip. He could do without the interruption to his normal routine. He was nearly finished with Max Brooks' *World War Z* and—

Ken stopped.

In the Superintendent's House, a flicker of light danced across the first floor, study window.

Really? Ken sighed. He took a long pull on his pipe and let it out slowly. He slipped the flashlight free from his belt and thumbed the power on. Ken played the beam along the old brick path as it led to the small front porch of the vacant Superintendent's home.

A sharp, brutal thaw had swept through the state at the start of the month and melted the snow. The cold had returned, of course, but the snow had held off. Saturday, perhaps, they might see a little, but not much.

Ken pushed thoughts of snow out of his mind as he neared the long, worn out stairs leading up to the front door. He moved the flashlight's beam onto the window where the foreign light shined, and then he brought it back to the porch.

The strange light continued to flicker around the room.

With a frown, Ken climbed the stairs. He winced at the sudden pain in his knees and hips. His heart beat angrily as he reached the door and Ken paused.

The door was ajar.

The doorjamb was splintered around the lock, the wood scraped deeply.

Ken tightened his grip on his flashlight before he pushed the door open.

It moved back on quiet hinges, and Ken saw the flicker of light beneath a closed door on the right. He took his pipe out of his mouth and breathed deeply.

"Hello," Ken called out. "You're trespassing. You need to come out of there."

A groan was the only response.

Ken sighed. "Listen, I'm not going to call the cops. I just want you to leave."

The groan was replaced by a sob and Ken's heartbeat quickened.

He went to the door, put his pipe back into his mouth, and rapped on the wood with the butt of the flashlight. A low moan joined the sob.

"Aw hell," Ken said. He twisted the doorknob and pushed the door in.

He stopped and looked, horrified at what he saw.

A pair of men hung suspended in midair. Nothing Ken could see had held them in place. They rotated slowly, their heads down, chins on their chests. Blood dripped from their noses and mouths, from cuts on their faces and leaked from their ears. The dark liquid tapped gently on the floor as it fell and splashed across broken plastic lenses.

Flashlights hung from straps on the men's wrists to create the flickering light Ken had seen from the road.

A scratching sound suddenly filled the air, drowning out the bestial complaints of the hanging men.

Ken played his own light across the walls until he saw words being scratched into the wall above the hearth.

Protect my Domain. Septimus Rex.

The men crashed to the floor, and one of them screamed as his bones broke with a harsh crack.

Ken's hand shook as he dug his cell phone out of his inner pocket and dialed 911 while the men writhed on the dust covered floor in agony.

Chapter 4
Getting Ready to Work

"I don't like it," Jenny said, handing him a tumbler of Jefferson's Bourbon.

"Thanks, Babe," Brian said, taking the drink and adjusting his position in his chair. "What's not to like about it?"

"What do you think?" she said. Her voice was harsh, and her eyes flashed with anger. "We haven't done any overnights since Sylvia died, Brian."

"I know we haven't," Brian said. "But we can't shy away from it."

"It's not shying away," Jenny snapped. She sighed and dropped into her chair. "Babe, it took you months to fully recover from the beating Paul gave you. And I still have nightmares about Sylvia. I know neither of those happened because you spent the night in Wells, but I don't like the risk. You were attacked there, not only by Paul but by another ghost too. And, not to sound too paranoid, but you're talking about spending the night in a sanitarium. So if there are ghosts, they might be insane."

Brian nodded. "I know. If there are people who haven't been able to move on we need to help them, though."

"Yes," Jenny said, looking at him. "But I can't spend the night, Babe. I can't."

"Okay," Brian said after a moment. He took a drink. "I'm not sure if I'm excited or nervous about this."

"Probably a little bit of both," she said. Jenny reached down, picked up her crochet work and turned the light on beside her. "When do you want to do it?"

"Tomorrow," he answered. "According to the real estate agent, there's a security guard on for each shift. The third shift guy is the best, I guess. He's been there for years. I'm planning on talking with him. Figure out if there are any particular hotspots."

"And you'll bring all of the equipment?"

Brian nodded. "I'll start packing soon. I want to leave around nine, nine thirty. Just to make sure I miss all the traffic up along route three."

"Just make sure you take the backup charger for your cell, okay?"

"I will," Brian said with a smile. "I really don't want to be stuck without any way to communicate with you."

"My thoughts exactly," she said. "You know, I've been thinking, we might want to hire someone to help with the tech stuff. I don't have a problem with the administration stuff, but I don't think I can really make myself investigate anymore."

He looked at her, concerned. "Sweetheart, do you need to stop altogether?"

Jenny shook her head. "No. I just won't go in the field with you. I... I can't."

"Okay," Brian said. "Do you want to look around, maybe get in touch with some of Sylvia's friends?"

"Yeah," Jenny said, sighing. "I'll send out some emails tonight. I'll let you know what's going on."

"Okay," Brian said.

CHAPTER 5
KEN, MIDDLEBURY SANITARIUM,
SEPTEMBER 2ND, 1969

Ken parked his pickup in the lot right outside of the guardhouse in front of the Middlebury Sanitarium. Behind the small structure loomed the buildings of the facility. Birds sang in the branches, the air smelled of autumn, and screams cut through the early morning chill.

Ken stood by the truck and listened.

He had heard screams before. Plenty of them. But there was a difference between men who were in physical agony from gunshot wounds and artillery versus what Ken was hearing now.

These cries were full of horror. Terror. Rage.

The cacophony hurt his ears.

An older man in a pressed uniform stepped out of the guardhouse and walked to Ken.

"Son?" the man asked.

Ken blinked then he looked at the man. "I'm sorry, sir."

The man smiled. "No worries, son. No worries. It takes most folks by surprise when they first hear the Factory."

"The Factory?" Ken asked.

"Inside joke," the man said with a tired smile. "You're Ken Buckingham?"

"I am," Ken said, offering his hand.

The man shook it. "Gus Delianos. You're here for the third shift position."

"I am."

"Come on with me," Gus said.

Ken followed him as Gus walked up to the guardhouse where another man around Gus's age sat with a newspaper.

"Alex," Gus said, "I'm taking Ken here on a quick tour."

Alex looked up, nodded, and then he returned his attention to the paper.

Gus chuckled and stepped back onto the main road. As Ken walked beside the man, Gus asked, "So, how long were you in?"

"Four years," Ken answered.

"Regular infantry?" Gus asked.

"Yes. You know," Ken said, "you're the only place to even give me an interview."

"Not surprised," Gus said. "When I got home from the Pacific in forty-seven, people wanted to just put the war behind them. And when they sent me off to Korea, hell, people didn't even know we were there or what was going on after that one."

"How long were you in for?" Ken asked.

"Two years in the Pacific," Gus answered. "Then the Corps activated my reserve unit and sent me back for another year in Korea. So, three altogether."

"Two wars."

"One war and a police action, if you listened to Truman. Which I didn't," Gus chuckled. "Anyway, I want to let you know this place gets a little strange after dark."

"How so?"

"Well, for starters, most of the poor folks in here get sedated for the night. Means it should be quiet, but it's not."

Gus came to a stop in front of the small house. The home was built of brick, and the curtains were drawn against the morning sun. The yard was well maintained, an apple tree neatly trimmed and heavy with fruit.

"This place," Gus said, gesturing to the house, "hasn't been occupied in years. Work here long enough and you'll find out why. My point, though, Ken is you'll see and hear things when you're doing your rounds. This house, this is one of the worst. Lights, voices, yelling, fighting. All of it."

Gus waved his hand around the campus. "You'll see people who aren't here. Might even talk to them. Might even be chased by them."

Ken looked at the older man and tried to see if Gus thought Ken was a rube.

Gus didn't.

The sincerity and concern in his eyes were shocking.

"I do all of the hiring when it comes to security, Ken," Gus said, looking at him steadily. "There's a reason why my boss tells me to choose combat vets. They're steady. They don't get the itch to bug-out. There's something bad here, Ken. Something real bad. We protect the residents as best we can. Not their fault they're loony. Hell, there are some boys here from the war, from Korea, and Vietnam, too. Even got a couple from the Great War. Uncle Sam may have shoved them in a corner, but we're not going to let them be in the dark if we can help it."

Ken looked around the grounds and tried to picture it at night. The lamps along the road would be lit. There would be night nurses in the buildings.

And Ken could feel something wrong, something bad in the air.

Something waiting for nightfall.

Ken looked at the older man. "When can I start?"

CHAPTER 6
AT MIDDLEBURY SANITARIUM

Brian arrived at the Middlebury Sanitarium at almost eleven o'clock in the morning. He let the car run and the heat blast as he stepped out into the cold January air. A skinny young man, bundled up against the cold, opened the door to a small guardhouse.

"Can I help you?" the young man asked. His voice had a thick, upstate New Hampshire accent.

"I'm Brian Roy," Brian said. "I was told you would be expecting me."

"I'm not the regular first shift guy," the guard replied. "Let me check with my boss, okay?"

"Sure," Brian said. "I'll be in the car."

The young man nodded and slipped back into the guardhouse.

Brian got back into the heat of the KIA, picked up his phone, and sent a quick text to Jenny. *This place is huge. I'm definitely going to need someone to help me with this.*

He sent the message and a few minutes later, as he still waited for the guard, Jenny's response came in. *Okay. Should be talking with Sylvia's niece, a girl named Anne. She and Sylvia were close. Be safe. Love you.*

I will. He put the phone away and took a drink of water.

A few minutes later the young man opened the guardhouse door and waved to Brian.

Brian got out of the car again and hurried up to the guard. "What's going on?"

"Come on in," the young man said, moving aside for Brian.

Brian squeezed into the small room as the young man closed up.

"My name's Derek, Mr. Roy," the guard said, taking off his glove and offering his hand.

Brian shook it. "Pleasure, Derek. Just call me, Brian, okay?"

"Sure thing, Brian," Derek said with a grin. "So, I just got off of the phone with Carl Reynard, my boss. I guess they got a house set up for you. It's the head nurse's old place. They set up a generator so you can have heat and power. You're staying the night?"

"I am."

"Damn," Derek said, shaking his head, "you're a brave man."

"Have you ever stayed the night?" Brian asked.

"Tried to. Once." Derek's face paled with the memory. "Didn't sleep well for a month. Still get nightmares about it. And hell, I went through the Kandahar Valley."

"You're a vet?"

Derek nodded. "All the security guards are. Kind of a tradition. Carl, his family, has been in charge of security at this place since it was first built. They only hire vets. But only combat vets, you know?"

"I do now," Brian said.

"Anyway," Derek said. "Place is scary as hell. Don't know how Ken does it."

"Who's Ken?" Brian asked.

"Third shift guard," Derek said, smiling. "Great guy. Retired a couple of years ago, but he still does it. Officially, he only works part-time. Unofficially, guy's here eleven to seven, seven days a week. I've never known him to take a night off."

"How long has he been doing it?" Brian asked.

Derek shrugged. "Couldn't tell you for sure. My old man, he says Ken was doing it when Carl took over the business from his father back in nineteen ninety."

"Hasn't he ever had a day off?" Brian asked.

"Nope. I asked my old man why Carl didn't make him and my father said something strange."

"What?"

"Well," Derek said, looking out the back window of the guardhouse at the sanitarium, "He said the place would come alive if Ken wasn't here to keep 'em quiet."

CHAPTER 7

KEN, FIRST NIGHT, 1969

"Ike Fenton," the man said, pausing to light a cigarette.

"Ken Buckingham," Ken said. He pulled out his new pipe, broke open his tobacco pouch and packed the bowl. He lit the pipe and dropped the match into an ashtray on the desk.

"Who were you with?" Ike asked.

"The one twenty-sixth Air Traffic Control," Ken said. "Crew chief on a Huey."

"What's that, kid?" Ike asked. "Last time I saw any military hardware up close was when they were strapping me to a Jeep in Korea."

Ken chuckled. "Huey. Helicopter gunship. You watch the news at all?"

"When I can't sleep."

"You see the guy hanging out the side of the helicopter wearing a helmet and behind the M-60 machine gun?"

"Yeah?" Ike asked.

"Look for me next time they show some old film."

Ike laughed.

"What about you?" Ken asked.

"Korea. Like I said. Fifth Regimental Combat Team. Best friend stepped on a landmine. Took a whole lot of shrapnel and wore a whole lot of him," Ike said.

"Sorry to hear it," Ken said.

Ike shrugged, tapped the head off of his cigarette and said, "Well, so much for the basics, huh? Ready for a stroll?"

Ken looked out at the sanitarium. The screaming of the residents had lessened significantly, as Gus said they would. The medications had been passed out.

The lights along the streets and paths had been turned on, and the sun was just beginning its descent behind the forest. The doctors had retired to their houses. The head nurse to hers. Orderlies and nurses had gone to their separate dormitories. The night nurses had taken their posts. A few other guards patrolled the grounds, and Ken was paired up with Ike to learn the ropes.

"Come on, Kid," Ike said. He took a pair of flashlights down from a shelf and handed one to Ken. "We'll be out until it's dark. Lot of ground to cover."

They left the guardhouse, and Ken walked alongside the older man. They followed the main road and occasionally caught sight of other guards.

"Why are they in teams of two?" Ken asked.

"We have to be," Ike said. "It's too dangerous not to."

"And not just from the residents?"

"No," Ike said, shaking his head. "I mean, yeah, you get the occasional resident who gets out, but it's the Factory we have to worry about."

"Why do you call it the Factory?"

Ike glanced at Ken, sighed and said after a moment, "Because this place, it makes things."

"What?" Ken asked.

Ike shrugged. "Don't rightly know how to describe them. Can you feel how the place is a little off?"

"It's a lot off," Ken answered.

"Exactly," Ike said in relief. "Was worried you wouldn't notice."

"I notice," Ken said. "So, what does it produce?"

"What you're feeling," Ike said. "It's worse at night. On our shift. Keeping the residents doped to the gills isn't so the night nurses can take some correspondence courses. It's so they don't get out onto the grounds. At night, right around three in the morning, we've lost some residents before. Even a guard once."

"What do you mean you lost them?" Ken asked, confused.

"Lost. Gone. No trace. Vanished." Ike stopped at a bench, stubbed out his cigarette on a piece of concrete furniture. "The joke, and it's a bad one, is this place makes ghosts. You know?"

Ken nodded.

"Now, this place is huge," Ike said, taking out a fresh cigarette and lighting it before continuing on with the tour. "We've got a kitchen facility, maintenance facility. Got a small infirmary. Pharmacy. Got a big old cemetery. I think the boneyard scares me the most. Anyway, got a post office and a library. Even a bus what runs to Concord, Manchester, Nashua, Boston, and back again. They get you fixed up with a room?"

"Xavier House," Ken answered.

Ike looked at him for a moment. "What room?"

"Three, on the first floor."

"Aw nuts," Ike said, spitting on the ground. "Who the hell put you in there, George?"

"George MacMillan," Ken answered.

"He ask if you were Army?"

"Yup."

"Hell, he's a squid. Navy guy. Hate's anybody who wasn't Navy. Well, at least, you'll be sleeping during the day," Ike said. "You keep to your new sleep pattern, okay? Don't you go trying to sleep at night. Not in room three."

"Why?"

"Mary," Ike said, looking at Ken through a haze of cigarette smoke. "She ain't overly fond of men."

CHAPTER 8
IN THE HEAD NURSE'S HOUSE

The head nurse's house was a tall, saltbox Victorian with a wide porch. The interior had been cleaned, and the water turned back on. A large, industrial generator hummed around the back of the house and broke the stillness of the air. Brian sat on a folding chair in an empty room and looked out directly through one of the tall thin old windows of the old building. A short but wide heater was plugged into the wall producing an impressive amount of warmth.

In a few minutes, he would bring in the equipment, take stock, and then figure out where to place them for the best results on the first night.

Brian looked out the window at part of the grounds. In the distance, trees barren of leaves and interspersed with evergreens spread out to the west. A few other buildings stood off to the left and a disturbingly large cemetery. A tall, wrought iron fence with pillars of granite between each section protected short, squat markers. From what Brian could see, some of the headstones were newer, others looked as old as the sanitarium.

The graves reminded him of home, of the sparsely populated burial ground in the basement of the house. His skin crawled at the memory of Paul, which dovetailed horrifically into memories of Wells.

Enough, he told himself, and he pushed the thoughts away.

He started to get up and paused. He watched as an older woman appeared from behind a headstone.

Literally appeared.

One minute the space had been empty, the next the woman walked towards the gate. Brian kept his eyes on her, and he wasn't surprised when she vanished as she stepped out of the cemetery.

Guess I'll be putting recorders out there, he thought.

He reached into his jacket pocket, took out a cigar and a lighter. As he walked to the front door, he lit the tobacco, and a heartbeat later it went out.

Brian stopped in the foyer, and he tried again. Just as the first smoke started to curl up towards the glass globe around the light, the cigar went dark once more.

The front door opened on its own accord.

"I'm sorry," Brian said, looking around the house. "I'll smoke outside."

He stepped out into the January cold, lit the cigar, and was pleased to watch it remain lit.

And I'll set a camera or two up in here as well.

Exhaling a large cloud of smoke, Brian walked to the car.

CHAPTER 9
INTRODUCTIONS ARE MADE

Ken hadn't needed an alarm clock for over thirty years. He woke up every day at four o'clock in the afternoon.

He never had to worry about being asleep when night fell.

By four thirty he was finished with breakfast, a shower, and had his uniform on for the night. If he needed to run errands, he did so. If not, he made his way to the Sanitarium's library. No one had ever bothered to remove the books. A tragedy, as far as Ken was concerned, but a boon at the same time.

There were over twenty thousand volumes. A large portion was extremely outdated medical and psychological texts, but there was still a healthy selection of literature. Newer stuff, like Brooks' zombie book, he picked up at the Middlebury tipping station. A small shed served as a place for people to put things they thought could be used again.

Ken was thinking about the tipping station when the phone rang.

Frowning, he walked over to it, took the handset off of the receiver and answered the call. "Hello?"

"Ken, it's Carl," Carl said.

"Carl, what can I do for you?"

"I've got a guest at the Factory tonight."

"What?" Ken asked, a chill sweeping through him. "Why?"

"Well, you know how the Gaiman Foundation is looking to buy the place?" Carl asked.

"Yeah?"

"Evidently they want someone to check the place for ghosts."

"Hell," Ken said, "place is haunted as hell."

"They don't want our opinion," Carl said with a sigh.

"So this guy's hired by the State?" Ken asked, frowning.

"By the State's real estate agent," Carl said. "From what I've heard the State's already irate."

"How come?"

"They wanted this guy to sign off and say the place was fine. Evidently he said he wouldn't."

Ken chuckled, smiling. "Okay. Maybe there's hope. Where is he?"

"I had Derek put him in the head nurse's old place."

"Why the hell did you put him there?" Ken snapped. "Jesus, Carl."

"What?" Carl asked, confused. "Where was I supposed to put him?"

"Hell, he could have crashed here with me. He shouldn't be on the grounds alone. You know better, Carl."

"Dan's there," Carl said defensively.

"And Dan's a good guy," Ken said. "He can't handle protecting someone, though, Carl. Damn it."

"Are you heading there, then?" Carl asked.

"Of course," Ken said angrily. "I'll be there in a few."

Ken hung up the phone and shook his head. He needed to get to the head nurse's house.

He took his small ring of master keys down off of the rack, slipped the leather strap connected to them around his belt and snapped it shut. He pulled on his coat and his pipe, tobacco, and matches went into his right pocket. He picked up his two-way radio, turned it on and tucked it into his breast pocket. A moment later he had on his watchman's cap and gloves, and he closed the door to his house.

A sharp wind cut down from the northeast and burned his nostrils, the scent of impending snow heavy in the air.

Bad storm coming, Ken thought, glancing up at the dark clouds rolling down from Canada. He had enough food stocked, of course, he was a born and bred New Englander. You didn't play with Winter. More often than not the Old Man would sweep down from the north and bury you. No matter what the weathermen said.

Ken zipped his collar to the top so it covered his chin and he quickly velcroed the protective flap over the zipper. He followed the brick path from his front door to the sanitarium's main road and he took it towards the head nurse's house.

The two-way radio squawked.

Ken grumbled and fished it out. He keyed it and said, "Go ahead, Dan."

"You on the main road?" Dan asked.

"Yup."

"Going to the library?"

"Not yet," Ken answered. "Just talked to Carl about the guest."

"Oh. Yeah. You know they put him in the head nurse's place?" Dan asked.

Ken rolled his eyes but kept the frustration he felt out of his voice. "Yup. Keep your ears open, Dan. I'll be by around eleven, just as always."

"Okay, Ken. Base out."

Ken put the radio away and as he followed a curve in the road, his destination appeared. In the stillness, the sound of the generator ripped through the air. Light spilled out from the windows of the dining room and reached for the cemetery.

Of all the damned places, Ken thought. He fought to keep his anger down. Carl did some stupid things, but he hadn't risked anyone's life before.

But does he even know he's risking this man's life? Ken asked himself. *Does Carl even understand? Really understand?*

Ken turned onto the walkway for the house and called out, "Hello, inside!"

He reached the stairs and hurried up them.

"Hello!" he called again.

The door opened, and a man in his forties stood there, framed by light. He was bald, solidly built and he wore a heavy sweater and jeans with work boots.

"Yes?" the man asked.

"I'm Ken Buckingham, third shift watchman here," Ken said.

"Hello," the man grinned. "Come on in. My name's Brian. Brian Roy. I was told you were the best person to speak with."

Brian closed the door behind Ken. Ken could see from the hall into the dining room. The man had an impressive array of laptops and wires set up on a folding table. It looked like something out of a movie. And Ken had no idea what any of it was for.

"I wasn't expecting to speak with you until after eleven," Brian said.

"I didn't know I was going to speak with you at all," Ken said.

Brian chuckled. "Figures."

"You know," Ken said, glancing around the house nervously. "This really isn't the best place for you to be set up."

Brian frowned. "How so?"

"Well, the last head nurse to live here doesn't particularly like company."

"No?" Brian asked with a chuckle. "I know she doesn't like smoking."

"You tried to smoke in here?" Ken asked.

Brian nodded. "She kept putting it out."

"Be happy she didn't do more," Ken said. "She's not the most patient woman."

"Real quick, Ken," Brian said, turning partially. "Is there someone who hangs around the cemetery?"

"Who did you see?" Ken asked after a moment.

"A woman," Brian answered. "She came out from behind a headstone and then disappeared at the gate."

"Come out of the house now, Brian," Ken said softly. "I want you to come out of the house."

Brian opened his mouth to answer, but then he closed it. He turned towards the kitchen and Ken heard it, too.

A scratching sound.

The door separating the two rooms was closed, but the noise was distinct. It rose up from near the floor.

And the door moved.

Ever so slightly it edged into the dining room, perhaps half an inch. Then it dropped back.

The scratches sounded again, and once more the door was pushed out.

A little further.

Enough to catch a glimpse of darkness.

Something sighed.

"We need to leave," Ken whispered. "Don't worry about your gear."

Brian nodded. He stepped into the dining room and took his coat off of the back of the chair.

A groan seemed to force its way into the room even as the door pushed outwards.

A hand grasped the bottom edge.

A pale, bloody hand. The nails were ragged and torn, flesh hacked and peeled back. As it held the door open, a second hand in a similarly miserable condition took hold of the jamb.

And a third and a fourth, and then a fifth.

Ken reached behind him, found the cold metal of the doorknob and twisted and pulled. Brian ran past him into the twilight and Ken followed.

Eleanor's shrieks chased them down the brick walkway.

CHAPTER 10

KEN, OCTOBER 12TH, 1970

Ken had seen and heard enough to understand a couple of things. The first was easy enough to accept. Ghosts did exist, and the sanitarium was haunted seven ways to Sunday. The second was a little harder.

The sanitarium was bad.

Not like a bad boy or a bad dog. Not even like a bad man.

But 'Bad' with a big old capital 'B'. Middlebury was wrong the way you read about in some of the papers from New York City and Boston. Wrong the way someone might kill another, and then decide to cook them up for dinner.

Wrong in the way the Indians used to torture their prisoners.

Wrong in the way the pilgrims sent blankets infected with smallpox as gifts to Indian tribes.

Twisted.

This place is twisted.

Gus had been right. They needed to protect the residents. Nearly everyone who worked there understood it. Not all, of course. Life would be too easy if everyone accepted it.

Gus generally helped weed those people out. And if he didn't, well, then Middlebury sure as hell did.

It was only a matter of getting the people out before they got hurt. Or someone else got hurt.

Ken and Ike leaned against the guardhouse and looked at Gus. Usually, they only saw him at the end of their shift, when he was coming in. Not at the start of it.

Something was wrong.

Gus looked angry.

"Here's the skinny," Gus said. "I spoke with Doctor Cushing this afternoon. A couple of the residents over in Building Two said they haven't been getting their meds. Also, we've got one of the catatonic girls on the fourth floor who looks like someone's using her as a plaything."

"Jesus Christ," Ike muttered. He took out a cigarette, lit it and exhaled angrily. "Any idea?"

"Yeah," Gus said, nodding. "Guy named Randy Briggs. He's been moved from second to third shift in Building Two. Usually, they try to rotate the shifts, or else stick someone on there they want fired, but this guy actually asked for third. Now you both know how crazy it can get, and Two's pretty damned bad."

"Did Doc find out about the meds the same time as the girl?" Ken asked.

"Yeah," Gus said. "The first shift super over there was told what was found with the girl, and so she went into the filing cabinet to see the girl's file. See if there was a problem with self-abuse or anything. When she was in there, she found the building's complaint file was all twisted around. She reached a little further back and found the complaints about the meds."

"Damn," Ken said.

"Yeah," Gus said. "This guy Randy's in pretty tight with the union steward, so Doc really wants us to catch him in the act. I already talked to the other guys, they're going to pick up the slack tonight for the patrols. I want the pair of you in Two. Doc's not worried about the meds. He had the second shift nurse give the three patients who've been getting shorted a little extra in case Randy skimps tonight.

"What Doc and I are worried about," Gus continued, "is Randy doing any more damage to the girl, or to a different one. You'll be able to stay in the super's office on the fourth floor. Keep your eye out for him."

"Kid gloves or full on, Gus?" Ike asked. The man's voice was low and angry.

"Full on," Gus said. "I'm okay with him meeting the judge with his jaw wired shut."

"Good," Ike grumbled, and Ken nodded.

Together they left Gus and walked to Building Two. Randy would be on the first floor, near the phone and the pharmacy. In wordless agreement, Ken followed Ike as the older man went to the back of the building. Ike unlocked the rear door, and the two of them quickly and quietly climbed the stairs.

When they walked onto the fourth floor Ken was covered in sweat, his undershirt and underwear soaked.

A smell of disinfectant swept over them, pushed by the giant fans which moved the air. The metal blades moved slowly as they hung from the dark ceiling. A few red lights glowed along the walls, between the windows and their bars.

The supervising nurse's office was on the left, and the door was ajar.

Ike opened it, and Ken followed him in. The desk was neat and orderly. A pair of plants stood on the window sill. Half a dozen tall filing cabinets stood off to one side, and a couch occupied the other wall. Ike pulled the curtain down behind the plants, and Ken turned the Venetian blinds on the door's glass so they could see out into the ward.

Forty beds stood in four neat rows. In each bed, a woman slept. Some of them fitfully. Some peacefully. A few of them could communicate, from what Ken had heard, but for the most part, these women had withdrawn completely from the world. A few had to be hand fed.

Ike sat behind the desk, and Ken found a chair by the door. He dragged the extra seat behind the desk to sit beside the older man.

"I'm going to beat the hell out of this boy," Ike said in a low, conversational tone. "Not a problem, is it?"

Ken shook his head. "Not at all, Ike."

"Didn't think so," Ike said. "Just wanted to check."

Silence slipped over them, and they sat and waited. Occasionally Ike would light a cigarette and keep the tip hidden behind his hand as he smoked. The hours passed by slowly and Ken shifted uncomfortably in his chair. He'd have to slip outside soon and use the bathroom, but he would wait a little longer.

The door opened at the far end of the ward. Light burst in from the stairwell and a shape slipped in.

Ike eased himself up out of the seat, and Ken did the same.

The figure stole forward and came to a stop near one of the beds. It reached out a hand to pull back the covers and something screamed.

Ken slapped his hands over his ears and staggered. Ike did the same, and then the man pointed, just as all of the lights turned on.

"Damn it!" Ken screamed, rubbing at his eyes. When he could see again, he saw Ike open the door, and Ken followed the man onto the floor.

A man dressed in a white orderly's uniform was suspended in the air. An unseen hand clutched the front of his shirt.

The man saw Ken and Ike and yelled, "Jesus, help me!"

And then he was thrown into the nearest window.

The man shrieked as the glass shattered and several of the bars bent slightly. Something picked the man up and hurled him into the bars again.

The man's screams increased and blood exploded out into the room.

The unseen thing continued to throw the man until the screaming stopped.

Ken and Ike could only stand and watch.

Finally, the man was lifted up and then dropped to the floor.

"*You*," a female voice said, and Ken could feel anger and hate directed towards them.

"Oh sweet Jesus," Ken whispered. Then, raising his voice, he yelled, "Run, Ike! Run!"

Ken grabbed hold of the older man and started to pull him towards the stairwell.

The unseen woman howled and chased after them.

Ken let go of Ike as they reached the door. They crashed through it and fell onto the stair landing. Ken bounced off the far wall, tripped, and fell down the first flight of stairs. He grunted as he felt some of his ribs crack. He groaned and rolled onto his back. Ike started down the stairs as the door to the fourth floor was torn off of its hinges and hurled backward. The unseen thing grabbed hold of Ike and with a howl threw him through the window on the landing.

The glass, wooden sashes and the iron bars all gave way at once.

Before darkness laced with pain swept over him, Ken saw Ike smile and close his eyes.

Chapter 11
In Ken's House

"Thanks," Brian said, accepting a mug of coffee from Ken.

"You're welcome." Ken sat down across from Brian at a small table. The older man reached up and took a bottle off of a shelf. Jamesons Whiskey. He opened it, poured a little into his coffee and looked at Brian. "You want to Irish it up?"

"Please," Brian said, nodding.

Ken added some to Brian's mug, capped the bottle and put it back. The man took a drink, looked at Brian and said, "You weren't too fazed by what you saw."

"No," Brian agreed.

"Seen the same before?" Ken asked.

"Not the same, but just as bad," Brian answered. "Are there more of those kicking around the sanitarium?"

"There are," Ken said after a moment. "Thing is, they've been quiet for a few years. They were still active right after the facility was shut down, but they've sort of gone to sleep, I guess. Not until the real estate agents and the buyer started tromping around did they wake up."

"They haven't reacted to the security guards?" Brian asked.

Ken chuckled. "I'm the only guard who patrols, Brian. The others only watch the gate. And the dead or whatever it is that lives here, well, they know me. They tend to leave me alone. Oh, every so often something happens, but it's rare."

"When's the last time something happened?" Brian asked. He took a drink of his coffee and enjoyed the pleasant heat of the coffee and the flush brought on by the whiskey.

"Two nights ago," Ken said.

Brian chuckled.

"Didn't say it wasn't recent," Ken grinned. "Only rare."

"Fair enough. What happened?"

The grin fell away, and Ken became serious. "We get these young people, you know, twenty-somethings. They like to do what they call urban spelunking. You heard of it?"

Brian nodded.

"Anyway," Ken said, shifting in his seat, "they like to come here. They think abandoned sanitarium, they read about the tunnels connecting the buildings. They figure minimal security. Sure, I can see how it would be exciting. It makes me work a little harder, and I worry about them. Middlebury isn't a good place to be in the daylight. Night time, Brian, night time is bad."

"So what happened two nights ago?" Brian asked.

"I started one of my walks," Ken said. "Patrolling the grounds. I saw a light in the superintendent's house. I went inside, and I found them hanging there."

"Found who?"

"A pair of brothers," Ken answered. "They'd been beaten up pretty badly. They were alive, though, which is more than the King usually allows."

"Wait," Brian said, holding up a hand. "The King? Who's the King?"

"I'm not sure," Ken said. He finished his coffee and set the mug aside. "He's been here as long as I have. He's not a happy man. Doesn't take kindly to strangers or uninvited guests."

Brian rubbed his chin. "It couldn't have been something the brothers had done for an internet stunt?"

Ken shook his head before he stood up and refilled his coffee cup. He added another dose of whiskey to it. "You want more of both?"

"Please," Brian said. He finished off his coffee and passed the mug up to Ken. The man filled it, added some whiskey, and handed it back to him. Brian wrapped his hands around the warm ceramic and then he asked, "What about the way they were hanging?"

"What about it?" Ken asked, sitting back down at the table.

"Was it a rope they used? Was it wrapped under their arms? Was it tied off to a beam? A piece of furniture?"

"No," Ken said. "You don't understand, Brian. They weren't tied with anything. They were simply hanging there. Suspended above the floor and

32

they dropped after I entered the room."

"Oh. Damn."

Ken nodded.

The man's two-way radio suddenly sounded off with a loud buzz.

Ken frowned, took the radio out of his pocket and said, "Go ahead, Dan."

"Ken, you still with the guest?" Dan asked.

"Yup."

"Where are you two?" Dan asked.

"My place. Why?" Ken asked.

"Oh. Well, ah, I just stepped out for a smoke, and when I came back, I saw a light on over by the boneyard."

"Where by the boneyard?" Ken asked, trying to keep his growing frustration out of his voice.

"The crematorium," Dan answered.

"The crematorium?" Ken asked. "Dan, there hasn't been any juice out there since before they closed the Factory down."

"I know. I thought it was a little strange."

"Alright," Ken said with a sigh. "Leave it be and stay in the guardhouse. No more stepping out for a smoke. Your shift's almost done, Dan."

"I copy," Dan said. "Base out."

Brian waited until Ken put the radio away before he asked, "Stepped outside for a smoke?"

Ken nodded. "Dan's a First Gulf War vet. Tanker. He lost most of his crewmates in a friendly fire incident. He smokes a lot of marijuana to keep his mind together. I don't ride him about it, but now I can't judge how long the lights been on at the crematorium. Dan's not exactly good about time when he's smoking."

"Understood," Brian said. He hesitated, thought about the thing in the head nurse's house, and then asked, "Well, do you want company to check out the crematorium?"

Ken looked at him for a moment. "If I say run, you run, though, Brian."

"I'll run," Brian said with a grin, interrupting him. "Don't you worry about it, Ken. I will run."

CHAPTER 12

KEN, MAY 13TH, 1975

Ken no longer had a partner.

He hadn't had one since Ike was killed. After the incident, he had asked Gus if he would be teamed up with someone else and the older man had shaken his head. When asked why Gus had handed him a note from Doc.

The King wants him to guard alone.

Ken wasn't sure who the King was, or why he wanted Ken to 'guard alone,' but evidently Doc and Gus played by the King's rules.

And so would Ken.

He was on his second pass of the night and he moved counter-clockwise. He had just passed the cemetery and the crematorium when the backdoor to the head nurse's house was thrown open.

Gloria ran down the stairs and into the yard. Hastily she pulled her dressing gown over her pajamas and Ken saw her feet were bare. Her dark red hair was up in curlers, and her pretty face wore a pinched expression.

"Ms. Sohn?" Ken asked, turning on his flashlight and pointing it down to the ground.

She turned around quickly, and her shoulders slumped slightly. "Oh thank God, Ken. Could you help me?"

"Of course," Ken said. He walked to her and once beside her asked, "What do you need?"

"I need Eleanor to stop what she's doing," Gloria said angrily.

Ken frowned. As the head nurse of the sanitarium, Gloria didn't have a housemate. And, as far as Ken knew, she wasn't a lesbian.

Maybe she is, Ken thought. He cleared his throat. "I'm sorry, Ms. Sohn, but who's Eleanor?"

She looked at him sharply, as if to see if he mocked her. When she was satisfied he wasn't, Gloria said, "Eleanor is someone who lives in the house and occasionally makes herself known."

Ken sighed. "A ghost?"

Gloria nodded.

"Where is she?"

"She's in the dining room," Gloria said angrily. "I got up to get a drink of milk and a piece of cake, and when I went in to eat, she was under the table. She kept pinching my legs and pulling my hair."

"Okay," Ken said. "I'll see if I can get her to calm down."

Gloria nodded and crossed her arms over her chest.

"Do you want to wait in the kitchen?" Ken asked.

"No," Gloria said, shaking her head. "She likes to stay in the pantry. I don't want to upset her if you actually get her out of the dining room."

"Fair enough," Ken said.

He left Gloria standing a few feet away from the back steps and entered the house. The kitchen light was on. A few dishes were in the drying rack. The refrigerator hummed loudly, and the air was warm. The radiator sputtered in a corner, and Ken walked quickly to the swinging door which separated the kitchen from the dining room.

Carefully he pushed his way in, the chandelier above the dark wood table lit. A soft light fell over everything, the neat rows of a blue and white dining service standing in a built-in china cabinet. A tall glass of milk and a plain white plate, occupied by a piece of chocolate cake and a silver fork were on the table in front of a pulled out chair.

The room was bitterly cold.

The shadow under the table was far darker than it should have been and Ken took a deep breath. "Eleanor?"

Something scuttled under the table.

"Eleanor, my name's Ken. Ken Buckingham. I'm a security guard here."

The chair across from him bumped against the edge of the table.

"I was wondering if I could ask you a favor."

Someone snickered. A cold sound which dug deep into Ken's stomach.

"Eleanor, Gloria would like to finish her cake and milk before going back to bed. Would it be alright for her to do so?"

The chair across from him started to slide out. An inch at a time it moved back, slowly and steadily. Once it neared the far wall, it came to a stop. A sickeningly pale hand snuck up around the edge of the table to grasp the wood. A second followed, and then a third, and then a fourth. Soon a fifth and a six were added, and Ken felt his heart begin to pound.

He could see the fingers tighten their grasp and a groan crept out from beneath the table.

Yet Ken stood still. He forced his breath to remain even.

The top of a head appeared. The hair was dirty, a mix of blonde and gray and black. Clumped together and wet.

A moment later a pale forehead, barren of any lines, followed the crown, and then the face appeared.

Eyes shifted from left to right, not in their sockets but in the face itself. Two eyes, then a dozen. Three, and then five. They moved around freely. The mouth was first normal, pale blue lips opening wide to reveal a dozen rows of teeth. The lips stretched and a pair of chins formed and separated.

The face was in constant motion.

And Ken could only watch as Eleanor straightened. She wore a stained white shift with arms pushing in and out of form. She stared at Ken with one eye and then with four.

"Eleanor," Ken managed to say. "Will you return to the pantry?"

She opened her mouth, and fresh blood slipped past the rows of teeth. A pair of tongues worked at her lips.

"I'm hungry," Eleanor said in a chorus of voices.

"Then go into the pantry," Ken said. His voice became stronger.

Eleanor snarled. "I'm *hungry.*"

"Go back to the pantry," Ken ordered.

Eleanor cocked her head to the left, smiled, and then she chuckled.

"Yes," she said. "Yes. I'll go to the pantry."

Eleanor disappeared.

For a moment, Ken stood there. He shook his head, turned around, and left the dining room. He passed through the kitchen, and into the backyard. Gloria stood where he had left her.

But her hair was gone, and she looked at him in shock, her eyes wide.

Gloria was as bald as a baby, and her red locks were nowhere to be seen.

"Ms. Sohn," Ken said gently. "Ms. Sohn, what happened?"

She looked at him, and whispered, "The King came."

"The King?"

"Yes. The King of the Factory," she said, still whispering. "Oh, Kenneth, the King. He liked my hair and so he took it. He liked my hair and he took it."

Ken took the radio off of his belt.

"This is Ken to base, over," he said.

"This is base, go ahead, Ken," came the response a moment later. It was Sean.

"Sean," Ken said, "can you send the ambulance to Ms. Sohn's house. We're around back."

"Emergency?" Sean asked.

"No, no blood or anything," Ken said. "But I need help."

"Okay. It'll be there in a minute, Ken."

"Thanks. Ken out."

Ken put the radio back and put his arm around Gloria's shoulders. He pulled her in and held her tightly.

She rested her head against his shoulder and said into the crook of his neck, "He liked my hair."

CHAPTER 13

HEADING TO THE CREMATORIUM

Brian pulled his hat lower and tried to ignore the biting cold in the January air. He kept his gloved hands in his pockets and walked beside Ken.

The old man set a steady pace. Quick enough to keep warm but not so fast as to break into a sweat. They followed a narrow path around the back side of the grounds. In the distance Brian could see the lights from the head nurse's house, and off to the left a soft glow.

"How long have you been here?" Brian asked.

"Since I got out of the army," Ken answered. "Nineteen sixty-nine."

"Were you in Vietnam?" Brian asked.

Ken chuckled. "Oh yes. Southeast Asia. My home away from home for thirteen months."

"Do you miss it?" Brian asked with a grin.

"Oh no. No, no, no, no, no," Ken laughed. "I still have nightmares about the place. Too hot. Too humid. Too many chances to get shot."

"What did you do?" Brian asked.

"Crew chief on a Huey," Ken answered.

"Damn. I had a friend who did the same thing. Guy named Lucky. Drank himself to death a few years ago," Brian said.

"Yeah," Ken said somberly. "Happened to a lot of guys I knew. Especially guys who did time in the firebases or saw a lot of action. Some got hooked on heroin in-country. Others simply drank when they got home. Anyway, enough sad stuff. What about you?"

"What about me?" Brian asked.

"How'd you get into this?"

"Looking for ghosts?"

"Yeah," Ken said.

"Well," Brian said. "My wife and I bought a haunted house."

"Why?" Ken asked.

Brian laughed. "We didn't know the house was haunted. We found out the hard way."

"Bad?" Ken asked, looking at him.

"Terrible," Brian said. After a moment, he added, "People died."

Ken nodded. "We've had a few of those here. It's why I'm a little concerned about all of this activity. Eleanor hasn't shown up since the late seventies, and the crematorium's been dark since eighty-two."

"Who's Eleanor?" Brian asked.

"You know the hands?" Ken asked.

"At the nurse's place?"

"Yup. Those are Eleanor's hands."

"All six?" Brian asked.

Ken nodded.

"Oh." After a moment, Brian asked, "Is the rest of her messed up, too?"

"Yes."

"Wow."

The cemetery came into view. The wrought iron fence, the granite posts, and the stones reflected the light of the house and the crematorium. Above them, the dark clouds looked heavy and angry. The light of the day bled out of the sky.

"Why would the light be on?" Brian asked after a minute as Ken led them to the building.

"I don't know," Ken answered. "I'm hoping it's nothing serious."

"Was Eleanor serious?" Brian asked.

"Compared to this," Ken replied, "no, she wasn't."

"Great," Brian muttered.

CHAPTER 14
SMOKES

Most of the time, Dan was pretty good with work.

He didn't stress too much. Really didn't have to deal with people. Hell, he just had to sit in a little box, keep an eye on the road and an ear out for the phone. Carl didn't care if he stepped out for a little weed for his head, and Ken was always there to help if needed.

Dan liked his job. Most of the time. Today was turning out to be a little different.

First, there had been a guest put in the head nurse's house, which was a bad call. All the shifts knew about the hotspots in Middlebury, and just because Eleanor had last raised her head when he was in high school didn't mean she wasn't around. Second, there was a light on in the crematorium. No juice to the circuits in there, but there was a light on.

Dan had caught sight of Ken and the guest walking from Ken's house towards the cemetery. And how Ken could live on the grounds was beyond Dan's ability to comprehend.

There was not enough grass in the world for Dan to remain calm while living in the sanitarium.

In fact, just thinking about it put a little itch in the back of his mind.

The itch would keep growing, Dan knew. Until he scratched it with a little marijuana.

And Ken had told him no more smoking. Dan knew Ken was looking out for him. Not because Ken thought grass was bad, but because something bad was happening on the grounds.

All the more reason to smoke, Dan thought.

His hands started to shake.

He couldn't smoke in the guardhouse. It was the only thing made clear by Carl. No one else wanted to smell the sickly sweet stench of Dan's weed.

I need a smoke, Dan thought. *Just one. I'll burn a quick one down.*

He went into his cooler, took out his stash of pre-rolled joints and grabbed his Bic lighter. He held onto them as he left the guardhouse and made his way to a tall hedge. Dan stood behind it, hidden from the road, and lit his smoke. He inhaled deeply, let out a quick cough and grinned up at the sky.

He slipped the lighter into a pocket and smoked a little more. He didn't mind the cold air, or the way clouds looked. Janet was supposed to come over, cook up some dinner and bring over some of the beer her brother brewed across the border in Vermont.

Dan took another hit off the joint and chuckled. He could feel his shins tingling.

Wonder if they added a little extra to this? He thought. The curious sensation spread from his lower legs up over his knees and down into his feet.

Dan went to wiggle his toes inside of his boots and found he couldn't.

Dan looked down at his boots.

Small, thin branches had wrapped around the leather and punched through it. They had woven themselves into the fabric of his pants, and as Dan watched he could see the branches making their way up his legs.

He dropped his joint and tried to step away from the hedge, but he was frozen in place.

Branches shot out from behind him and lashed his arms to his side. Something slid up into his hair and curled around his head. It jerked him backward while another slipped in between his lips and burst out under his chin. Dan tried to scream, but more branches raced along his flesh to assault his mouth.

They pushed deep into his throat, and the last thing he felt were the branches burrowing down into his stomach.

CHAPTER 15
ASHES TO ASHES

Brian waited to the left of the crematorium's door while Ken unlocked it. He shivered, stamped his feet, and wondered why it had gotten so cold.

You know why, Brian told himself.

And he did.

"Ready?" Ken asked, glancing over at Brian.

"Yes," Brian said.

"Okay," Ken said, putting his keys away. "Remember what I said before. I say run, you haul out of here like a jackrabbit. You get right to your car, and you get going."

"You got it."

Brian watched as Ken turned the knob and opened the door.

An old, terrible stench of burnt flesh seeped out of the building. A narrow corridor, dimly lit with light from an open doorway far down on the right welcomed them.

The soft tones of an intimate conversation accompanied the smell, and Brian stepped nervously into the crematorium. Ken left the door open and took the lead. Brian followed him down the hall. They came to a stop and looked into the open room.

Along the left wall stood the heavy iron slide which could be opened and closed. Beyond it, excised organs and amputated limbs would have normally been burnt. A single window dominated the far wall and lacked a curtain. It was the object in the room's center, however, that caught Brian's attention.

A round table with a marble top. Elegantly curved and carved legs which looked surprisingly delicate supported the stone. A trio of men stood around it. They were older men, their white hair clipped to brush the edges of the collars on their white coats.

Before each man was a plate, and upon each plate were various meats. A bottle of wine accompanied each place setting, and a wine glass as well. The men chatted pleasantly with one another, occasionally one would pause, cut a piece of meat and eat it. The unknown flesh looked barely cooked as blood fell from it easily.

One of the men looked over, his lips dark from either blood or wine.

"Kenneth," the man said. "You've brought a friend."

The other two men continued their own conversation, something, Brian realized, which concerned how best to secure a man's precious bodily fluids. They ate precisely and delicately.

"Gentlemen," Ken said, and Brian heard the nervousness in the older man's voice. "May I ask what you're doing here?"

The one who had spoken chuckled. "Eating, Kenneth. Eating. We find it easier to eat this meal here than in our own homes."

The man's partners nodded in agreement even as they continued their talk.

"You do know the crematorium is closed?" Ken asked.

"No," the speaker said, honestly surprised. "We did not. It's so rare we get to eat anymore. Especially like this. There was a time, Kenneth when Middlebury was extremely productive. We ate like this every week. Delicacies such as you couldn't imagine."

"What are you eating?" Brian asked.

The speaker smiled slyly. "Incredibly fresh meat. A liver. A pair of kidneys. Mm, and a tongue. Again, rarities now."

"From what?" Brian asked even as Ken took a step back.

"Not from what," the speaker chuckled. "From whom."

"From whom then?" Ken asked.

"Well, Kenneth," the speaker said, "I am not aware of the gentleman's name. One of your coworkers. He had a disturbing habit of smoking far too much cannabis than I would have prescribed."

Ken stiffened. "You'll have to leave."

"Once we're finished," the speaker said. He looked at Brian. "Is he staying long, Kenneth? He looks as though he might be rather tasty."

Brian didn't wait for Ken to tell him to run.

He turned and ran.

In the hallway Brian slipped, stumbled forward and crashed into a wall.

He fell and smacked the floor heavily. He staggered out of the building, fell down and rolled onto his back.

Snow fell on his face, and Ken knelt beside him.

"Brian," Ken said. "Brian, are you okay?"

Brian nodded and let out a groan. His body ached. "Everything hurts, though."

He struggled to sit up, and Ken helped him.

The light was out in the crematorium.

"Are they gone?" Brian asked.

"I don't know if they're gone," Ken said grimly, "but I think they're done eating for now. Think you can walk?"

"Got to," Brian said. He tried to take a step and suddenly pain exploded through him.

He bit back a scream as his eyes threatened to implode. Something pushed in his head, as though a great force wished to enter, to crush his brain within his skull and fill it with itself. He swayed on his feet, pressed his hands against his eyes and choked back vomit.

A gift, a stranger's thought invaded his own. *A gift*.

The pain became manageable and Brian dropped his hands and looked around.

Leo? Brian thought, searching within his thoughts.

Yes, he had heard Leo's voice.

But what gift? Brian thought. And then he stood, shocked at what he saw.

"Oh Jesus," Brian whispered.

"What is it?" Ken asked. "What's wrong?"

"The dead," Brian said. "I can see the dead. They're everywhere."

Chapter 16
The Residents of Middlebury Sanitarium

Brian's head pulsed with pain. He stood just outside of the crematorium with Ken to his left. In front of Brian, however, and in his peripheral vision, Brian saw the dead.

Not one or two.

Not a dozen, or two dozen.

Perhaps a hundred. Maybe even more.

The blood in his veins threatened to push his eyes out of their sockets.

A few of the dead observed him with interest and curiosity.

Only a few, though.

The others were mad.

All of them.

Some shook where they stood, arms and legs uncontrollable. They nodded their heads far too quickly while even more squatted on the ground and rocked back and forth.

"Is there a safe place here?" Brian asked.

"My house is the safest place on the grounds," Ken said.

"I need to get there. Please."

Some of the dead stepped towards him. All of them were silent. Brian felt like he had walked into a conversation he shouldn't be a part of.

"Stay close." Ken said.

"You got it," Brian answered. He took his gloves off and stuffed them into his pockets, and then he put his hands in as well.

He needed his rings free.

Ken walked quickly, and then he groaned and started to limp.

"Are you okay?" Brian asked.

"Fine," Ken said through clenched teeth. He pressed a hand to his right hip and kept moving along the path.

Snow started to fall, and the dead closed ranks. One ghost took the lead. A middle-aged man dressed in a security guard's uniform. He moved close enough for Brian to read the name tag.

Fenton.

"Going to Ken's place?" the ghost Fenton asked.

"Yes," Brian answered.

"What?" Ken asked.

"Talking to a ghost, Ken," Brian said.

"What? Oh. Okay."

Fenton chuckled. "He's a good boy. A little older now. You tell him Ike says hello, alright?"

"Yes," Brian said.

"And you let him know," Fenton said, his voice becoming grim, "we never leave this place. Never. The King is waiting for him, Brian. The King is waiting, and he grows impatient."

CHAPTER 17

KEN, MAY 11TH, 1980

Something wasn't right.

Ken stood still near the rear entrance to the cemetery. He turned the volume down on the new handheld radio he had been issued, and closed his eyes. He listened, and waited.

His heartbeat slowed and kept a smooth, steady rhythm. A chill wind moved swiftly around him and carried with it the sweet smell of rain. A few cries and screams worked their way out of the various buildings, normal for Middlebury. Yet the sound he had heard, the noise Ken waited to hear again, it hadn't been part of the night's tableaux.

Ken let his body relax.

He could wait.

Middlebury had taught him to be patient. The Sanitarium had shown him how to talk peacefully with a disturbed resident who had escaped the confines of their room. Ken had learned to let dark shadows pass and leave some questions unanswered.

This sound, though, was different.

And it repeated. From the boneyard.

Ken opened his eyes and walked into the cemetery. He moved towards the noise.

"Why are you here, Kenneth?" a voice asked.

He paused and tried to identify it.

Male.

Ken continued on his way. A tall obelisk took form, released slowly from the shadows.

"Kenneth," the voice said again. "Don't you want to know how I am privy to your name?"

Ken kept his eyes on the monument.

"Everyone knows my name," Ken said. "Why shouldn't you?"

Something cold raced past him, ripping the breath from his mouth.

"I'm not anyone," the voice said, coming from ahead of Ken. "I'm everyone. All of them. All of you."

"How long have you been here?" Ken asked, after he caught his breath.

"Longer than most. Less than some."

"Not helpful at all, chief," Ken said. He turned slightly. He wanted to come up at an angle on the obelisk.

The voice chuckled happily. "It wasn't meant to be."

"Oh," Ken said.

"What are you looking for, Ken?" the voice asked.

"Whatever made the noise," Ken answered.

"Ah, you heard the birthing," the voice said. "You heard it being born."

Ken stopped a dozen yards away from the stone. "What did I hear being born?"

"Agony. Regret. Shock. Horror," the voice said. "All of these things. Everything dark and terrible. A purity. Is it not so?"

"I don't know about pure," Ken said. He took his radio out, turned the volume up and keyed it. "Ken to base."

"This is base," Cole said. "Go ahead, Ken."

"In the boneyard, Cole," Ken said.

"Resident?"

"Not this side of the grave."

Cole paused, and then he answered, "Do you need assistance?"

"No, just giving you my location," Ken said, eyeing the obelisk warily. "Just in case."

"Yeah, I copy, Ken," Cole said. "Give me a shout in five, alright?"

"Yup," Ken said. "Out."

Ken put the radio back. He waited for the voice to chime in, but the ghost didn't.

Okay, Ken thought, taking a deep breath. *Let's see what we have.*

Ken didn't give himself a chance to think twice. Instead, he moved quickly to the side of the obelisk, and then he came to a sharp, sudden stop.

A child sat on the grass and looked up at him.

A little girl. Perhaps six, maybe seven. Her hair was blonde and ragged.

Black circles under her eyes and the irises nearly swallowed by the pupils. Blue veins moved beneath her pale skin, and she wore a white hospital gown. In her hands, she held a stuffed toy. A black and white terrier.

The girl's eyes never left his face.

The wind picked up and blew her hair into her thin face. She tucked the wayward strands behind an ear.

Jesus, Ken thought. He squatted down and smiled at her. "Hello."

She smiled back at him, her teeth nearly translucent.

"My name's Kenneth."

"I know your name!" she suddenly snarled, and Ken fell back onto his rear.

The girl leaped to her feet and dropped her animal. She clenched her fists and bit her lip hard enough to draw blood. "We all know your name, *Kenneth*."

Ken tried to get to his feet, but she screamed at him again. The sound punched him in the chest, and he landed spread-eagle on his back.

The girl jumped towards him, and Ken rolled out of the way.

She roared in fury and twisted to face him.

Ken got to his feet and tried to gather his thoughts.

She didn't give him time to.

She opened her mouth and howled. The headstones around him exploded, and Ken screamed as they struck him. Something burned in his right hip, and he bit back on a second scream as it threatened to burst his throat.

He could feel blood rushing down his leg as he collapsed.

The girl dropped down low, stayed on her feet and fell forward onto her hands. She crawled towards him. Blood dripped from her lip as she grinned at him.

"Kenneth. *Kenneth*," she laughed. "Yes. I know your name, Kenneth."

Her body faded slowly until nothing remained.

Ken bit back the pain, forced himself to sit up and took out the radio. He keyed the handset, found he couldn't speak, and he hit the button five more times.

Five was his emergency number.

"On our way, Ken," Cole said.

Ken dropped the radio and looked around him. Three headstones were shattered. Granite littered the grass. The girl's stuffed terrier lay by the obelisk. The toy had a collar around its neck, and a tag caught the moonlight.

He could see a word etched upon the dog's medallion, and he squinted in the light to read it.

Kenneth.

CHAPTER 18

IN KEN'S HOUSE

They sat in silence.

At Brian's request, Ken pulled the blinds down and turned on all of the lights. There was no television to turn on. No radio. The small house was clean and austere with a few books scattered about.

Brian could hear the dead whispering through the walls.

"How are you holding up?" Ken asked.

"Trying to get a grip on it," Brian said. "It's strange."

"I can imagine," Ken said. He grunted as he shifted his right leg and put it up on the footstool.

"Are you okay?" Brian asked the older man.

Ken grinned and nodded. "Old injury."

"Work related?" Brian said.

"Yes," Ken answered. "Yes, it is."

"Do you mind if I send a text?" Brian asked.

"No," Ken chuckled, "but thank you. You know, I see people with their phones in town all of the time. Seems like they never stop."

"Yeah," Brian said. "I have to watch myself with it. Gets addictive."

He took the phone out of his coat and sent a quick text to Jenny.

Hey, Babe, this place is hot. Any help on the way? Want to get the gear set-up and safe home as soon as possible. Love you.

Several more minutes of silence passed between Brian and Ken before Jenny's response came through.

Be safe. Anne will be there in the morning. I gave her your number, Babe. BE SAFE. I love you.

"Everything okay?" Ken asked.

"Yeah," Brian said, putting the phone away. "I'll be getting more help in the morning."

"You're not leaving?" Ken asked, surprised.

Brian shook his head.

"Why not?"

"I've got to finish documenting this place," Brian said.

"You haven't got enough?"

"I don't even know what I have from the nurse's house," Brian said. "Probably won't be able to check it until the morning. I need to capture evidence, though, and I want to set up at the cemetery and the crematorium."

Ken sighed, rubbed the back of his head and then he said, "We'll want to get you into the library then."

"Is it active in there?" Brian asked.

Ken gave him a tight smile. "Yes. Yes, it is. Now, if you'll excuse me, I have to call in about Dan."

Brian nodded, and Ken stood up and walked gingerly to the kitchen. The man closed the door behind him.

Brian leaned his head back and closed his eyes. *They're so strong here.*

His stomach rumbled, and visions of the feast in the crematorium flashed in his memory. Brian's desire to eat fled.

With a groan, he opened his eyes and straightened up. The pain in his head settled into an angry grumble, and he wondered if the house was truly safe.

A few minutes passed and then Ken opened the door.

"I just called, Carl," Ken said as he sat down. "They're sending out a search team, but they won't find anything."

"Nothing at all?" Brian asked.

Ken shook his head.

"Others have disappeared?" Brian said.

"Yes," Ken answered. "Over the years. Here and there."

"Always guards?" Brian asked.

"Lord no," Ken sighed. "A few. Isabella still has several of them, at least I think she does. She keeps their spirits trapped in her house. And, Brian, Isabella, she's terrible. She won't give up the ones she's taken. Others have been killed. Guards, and residents alike. "Mysterious deaths," according to the State Police. My first and only partner here, his was listed as mysterious."

"Why?" Brian said.

"Well," Ken said, tapping the arm of his chair, "he somehow managed to throw himself out of a fourth-floor window."

"And him going out a window was mysterious?"

"It had bars on it," Ken said evenly.

"Oh," Brian said, and then he added, "did you know a man named Ike Fenton?"

Ken stiffened. "Yes, I did. Why?"

"I was talking to him on the way here. He said to tell you something about the King. But my head's fuzzy," Brian said, shaking his head to emphasize the point, "and I can't remember exactly what it was."

"The King?" Ken asked in a low voice.

Brian nodded.

"You better get what you need and get it done tomorrow, son," Ken said. "If the King's coming back, well, there's going to be hell to pay."

"Who is he?" Brian asked.

"He's the King," Ken said. "The Sanitarium is his, and through his faithful he rules with an iron fist."

CHAPTER 19
BUILDING THREE, MIDDLEBURY SANITARIUM, NOVEMBER 2ND, 1982

Ken shook the match out and dropped it into the ashtray by the bench. He took several long pulls on the pipe to make sure it was lit, and he enjoyed the fine, full flavor of the Virginia blend. Gus had brought it back from visiting his grandchildren in Washington, DC and Ken was extremely thankful.

"Ken!" Sean's voice barked from the radio.

Ken rolled his eyes, took the pipe out of his mouth and said, "Go ahead."

"Are you near Building Three?"

"No," Ken said, becoming alarmed and looking out over the property. "What's wrong?"

"The alarms are going off on the doors and no one's answering the phones."

Ken started to jog in the direction of Building Three. "Where are the other two teams?"

"Still chasing down the kid who got out of Building Two half an hour ago," Sean said, a note of panic creeping into his voice. "Their radios are here, Ken."

"Why are their radios there?" Ken asked, but even as the question formed he knew the answer.

Middlebury wanted the radios there.

Middlebury had let the teenager out to run loose.

Middlebury knew Ken patrolled alone.

Ken started to run. "On my way!"

He held onto the radio in one hand and the pipe in the other. Tobacco embers trailed behind him. Each flared for a brief moment.

Ken passed Building Four, and he heard the laughter from it. On the fourth floor, he caught a glimpse of something in the window, and he ignored it. Ahead of him, Building Three was brightly lit, and then it plunged into darkness.

A shadow swallowed it completely, and then a light appeared at the bottom.

A door had opened.

Someone waited for Ken.

He aimed himself at the door.

Screams erupted from the darkened building and far behind him Ken heard malicious laughter. The nameless little girl from the cemetery stood beneath an elm tree, stuffed terrier in her hand.

She glared at him and wept tears of blood in her rage.

And then Ken was in Building Three.

The door closed gently behind him.

He stood in the foyer and saw why no one had answered the phone.

The night orderly stood by the elevator. He had been stripped bare, his skin pale white and sickly beneath the fluorescents. A radio played static and just beneath the noise Ken could hear voices. Some of the words he understood, many more he did not.

Evidently the orderly had heard them as well.

He had driven pencils into each eardrum.

The man was dead, yet how he managed to remain upright was a mystery until Ken stepped closer.

It looked as though the man had cut his own belt loop into his skin and slipped his belt through the hole in his flesh. The leather had then been slipped around the art deco ashtray built into the wall.

Yet the corpse…

No, Ken thought. *His name was Chuck.*

Chuck's wounds were bloodless. Not the slightest drop or even a hint of the life fluid. Ken reached out, touched the man, and found Chuck was frozen solid.

The door to the stairwell burst open, and a fresh series of screams rolled down the flights of stairs.

Ken ran through the open door and up the stairs. He followed the screams until he found his way onto the third floor. He stepped into the darkness, unable to distinguish anything.

He managed to gain control of his breath, put his radio back on his belt, and relight his pipe.

The match's flame illuminated only his hand and the briarwood bowl, which had remained miraculously half-filled.

"Ah," a soft male voice said. "My watchman has arrived."

Ken nearly choked.

"Will you not greet your King, Watchman?" the King asked, an edge to his voice.

Ken remembered his interview with Isabella in the House.

"My Liege," Ken managed to say, taking his pipe out of his mouth.

"Ah, you do not disappoint, Watchman," the King said in a purring tone. "Isabella was right. She knew I would be pleased with you."

The voice moved, circled around to the left. Ken stood and listened and waited.

"Too long," the King continued. "Too long have I suffered them here, Watchman."

Ken drew a long pull on the pipe, and then he let the strong smoke out slowly.

When the King spoke again, it came from behind him.

"You have been here for some time now?" the King asked.

"Thirteen years, my Liege," Ken answered.

"An auspicious number. I have," the King chuckled, "been here slightly longer than you. Slightly longer than, well, longer than all of them. Even Isabella, she was here before the first of them."

Ken clamped onto the stem of his pipe with his teeth and stuffed both of his hands into his pockets to keep them still.

"So," the King whispered, his voice at Ken's ear, "what shall we do with them?"

"My Liege?" Ken said around the pipe.

The King spoke from the front.

"These people here."

"The residents?"

"Warts. Growths. Leeches without the benefit of cure. Suckling pigs draining the life of my home," the King snapped. "Yes. Your 'residents.' What shall I do with them?"

"Leave them, my Liege," Ken said. He took the pipe out of his mouth. "Leave them."

"No, Watchman. You are too tenderhearted by far. You must not be. I come to sit upon my throne. I have been gone long enough. I will see them all like this."

The darkness vanished, replaced by a light so bright it caused Ken to cry out in pain and close his eyes for a moment. He blinked and then kept his eyes open to look at the ward.

The ceiling tiles had been removed and were neatly stacked by the ends of beds. Some pop song by the Jackson Five played on the radio at the nurse's station. The nurse stood on the desk, a numb look of horror on her slightly pudgy face. She had a sheet wrapped around her neck, the other end of it tied off to an exposed rafter.

"Look what I did," she whispered. "Don't save me."

And she stepped off of the desk.

Ken started towards her, but he saw her eyes bulge and tongue thrust forward from between her lips. He heard the crack of her neck and saw the mad tap of her feet on the air.

It was then he noticed the others.

All of the others.

Above each bed hung a resident. Some sixty women, and each of them had been hanged.

The room stank, not of bleach or cleansers. Not of the Virginia Slims the nurse, Karen, would smoke on her breaks.

It stank of death.

The ward smelled of the King.

CHAPTER 20

MEETING THE NEW HAND

Brian awoke at seven in the morning. It took him a moment to realize where he was, but he did so as he sat up and stretched. From another room, he heard snoring.

Ken, Brian thought.

Brian stood up, walked into the small kitchen and ran the tap for a moment to get some cold water. He found a glass in a drying rack and filled it. He stood at the counter and looked out at a wide expanse of fresh snow.

The dead watched him.

Perhaps a score of them. Brian didn't bother counting. He finished the water, quickly washed the glass and returned it to the drying rack. On the small dining table, he found a notepad and pen. Brian wrote a quick note to let Ken know he was going to go back to the head nurse's place to check on the gear.

With the information written down, Brian got his winter gear on and left the house. He closed the door quietly behind him. When he stepped down the few stairs to the brick path, Brian turned his collar up and tugged his hat down a little lower. Someone had shoveled out the walkway and plowed the road.

And a young girl stood on the cleared asphalt and watched him.

She was pale and dressed in tatters. In her hands, she held a stuffed animal, a dog of some sort. Her eyes locked onto him, and Brian knew he couldn't avoid her.

"Hello," he said as he drew closer.

She glared at him, her brow furrowed and her lips thinned.

"Have you come to walk with me?" he asked her.

"You were with Kenneth," she said.

"I was."

"Why?" she demanded.

"I needed to rest," he answered.

She sneered. "You could have rested with me."

"Where do you live?" he asked.

"The boneyard. The cemetery. Yes," she smiled, showing him a smile full of sickly teeth, "you could have rested with me."

"Thank you."

Brian started walking along the road, back towards the head nurse's house.

The dead girl went with him.

"The King likes His watchman," she said after a moment.

"Do you?" Brian asked.

"I hate him," she answered.

"Why?"

"Because I can."

A few minutes passed, and she added, "I think I like you."

"Thank you," Brian said.

"The King won't."

"Why?" Brian asked.

"Because the King only likes two people. One alive, and one dead," she said.

"The Watchman is one," Brian said. "Who is the other?"

"Isabella," the girl laughed. "And she likes everyone."

"She's friendly?"

"Not unless she has to be," the girl said wickedly. "And she wants to meet you, Brian Roy."

Brian looked down, and the girl was gone.

He shivered once involuntarily and hurried on towards the head nurse's house. He soon saw his car and a second vehicle parked behind it. Exhaust spilled out of the tailpipe of the unknown car, and Brian could see someone sat in the driver's seat.

Suddenly his phone rang.

Brian stopped, took the phone out of his pocket and looked at the number.

An unknown caller with a New Hampshire area code.

"Hello?" Brian asked.

"Is this Brian?" a young woman asked.

"It is."

"Hi Brian, my name is Anne, Anne Purvis. I'm Sylvia Purvis's niece," the young woman said.

"Oh, hey," Brian said. "Is that you parked in front of my car at the head nurse's house?"

"Yeah. I just knocked on the door, but no one answered."

"I'm walking up right now."

He saw her head turn in the driver's seat even as she said, "Oh, there you are. Bye!"

"Bye," Brian said, chuckling. He ended the call and put it away. Within a few moments, he was close enough to the car, and Anne shut the engine off and stepped out.

Her beauty nearly took his breath away.

She had short red hair peeking out from beneath a bright white knit cap. Her skin was pale, her lips bright red, and her eyes an impressive dark blue. Her face was elfin with her chin coming to a delicate point. She was bundled warmly against the cold, and she was short, even in the heeled knee-high boots she wore.

Anne was a miniature doll, probably barely old enough to drink, and Brian's heart beat a mad rhythm against his chest.

He cleared his throat nervously. "Hi Anne, I'm Brian."

"A pleasure," she said, smiling at him. Her teeth were a bright white, with a hint of crookedness to several of them. The cold wind carried a sweet smell, reminiscent of musk, to his nose.

Brian repressed a shiver.

"Do you want to go inside?" he asked.

"Please," Anne said. "It's freezing out here."

"Well," he said, "we may not be able to stay long inside, but it'll be warm, and we'll get the gear quick as we can."

"Why can't we stay long?" she asked, following him up to the front door.

Brian shook his head. "I'll tell you inside, Anne."

He held the door for her, glanced at the few ghosts who watched from the porch of another residence, and then he hurried into the house.

CHAPTER 21
ANNE GOES TO WORK

Brian led Anne cautiously into the dining room of the head nurse's house. From what he could see, all of the equipment was still there. All of the 'power' lights were green on the gear. The generator thrummed behind the house, the sound muffled by the new snow.

"Are you okay?" Anne asked, looking at him.

Brian gave her a tight smile. "Yes. Yesterday afternoon we had to leave here quickly."

"I thought Jenny said you were investigating alone?" Anne said.

"I am. Or, rather, I was. Yesterday the third shift security guard stopped by and we discovered our presence wasn't welcomed."

"By a ghost?" Anne asked, her eyes widening slightly.

"Eleanor," Brian said with a nod. "We need to gather up the gear as quickly as possible. After that, we'll go on up to Ken's place and look through the recordings. Sound good?"

"Yes," Anne said, looking around the room. "Is Eleanor going to come back?"

"I hope not," Brian said, hurrying to the table. "If she does we'll need to run. And I literally mean run. Most of the dead aren't particularly pleasant here."

"Okay," Anne said, and she stepped up to the table.

In silence, they started to disconnect the various devices. Anne quickly figured out which hard-cases went with each piece, and Brian didn't worry about the recorders he had set up in the cemetery.

Within fifteen minutes the two of them had gathered up every item. Brian left the chair, and the table behind as the two of them exited the house. With Anne's help, they carried the cases back up the road. They entered Ken's house quietly. Anne managed to close the door without the slightest bit of noise, and Ken continued to snore uninterrupted.

Brian led Anne into the kitchen, and they set the gear down by the backdoor.

"Go ahead and sit down," Brian said in a low voice, nodding towards the table.

Anne flashed him a smile which left him stunned and took off her winter coat and gloves. Her slim body was sharply defined by a tight gray sweater and she sat down with a delicacy and grace Brian had never seen before.

Swallowing dryly, he forced himself to focus on the laptop. He managed to get it out of the case, along with its power cord, and he plugged it into an outlet by the sink. He carried the computer to the table, opened it and powered it up. As the interior fan kicked in and hummed, Brian sat down across from Anne. He adjusted the position of the laptop, so they both could view it.

"Well," Brian said, "while we wait for this bad boy to load up, tell me why you took the job."

Anne gave him a wicked grin. "I was always interested in what my aunt did. Most of the family thought she was kind off of her rocker, but I didn't. When she passed away, I was upset, and I really wanted to learn more. I reached out to Jenny, and she told me she'd let me know."

"And she did," Brian said.

"She did," Anne smiled. "Anyway, here I am. I have absolutely no idea what to do, just so you know."

"Fine with me," Brian said. "For right now, it's going to be pretty boring. We'll watch the different videos recorded by the cameras. Then we'll check out the individual tracks for the digital audio recorders. If, or when we actually see something, we'll mark it for further review and keep on moving. Got it?"

Anne nodded. "Got it. Sounds easy enough."

"I'm hoping it will be," Brian said. "This place is haunted as hell, but we just need some evidence. Later on, I want to check out the library here too. More than likely Ken will have a key, and I'd feel better about going with him anyway."

"Why?" Anne asked.

"This place is scary," Brian said, looking at her. For a moment, he contemplated how she might react to the knowledge of how he could see the dead. *No. Not yet.* "So, are you ready?"

"Yes I am," she said.

"Okay," Brian said. He turned to face the computer, pulled up the first file and started it.

Camera One, placed in the foyer of the head nurse's house, popped up. Time moved by slowly. Eventually, Brian showed up on the screen, let Ken in and the two of them went into the dining room. A few moments later they ran out.

"What happened there?" Anne asked.

"I'll tell you later," Brian said. He opened his mouth to say more, and then he closed it.

Darkness crept into the foyer.

Brian hit the key to mark the time and waited.

A hand stole out of the deep shadow. The flesh upon the hand was pale, torn, bloodied. Anne inhaled sharply beside him.

The fingers groped along the wall. They seemed to pull the entire shadow along with it. Soon the darkness filled the camera, and Brian could see nothing.

Long minutes passed before the shadow slipped away.

"Oh Jesus," Anne hissed.

Brian could only nod his agreement.

Words had been written upon the plaster. Each letter was thick, seemingly burned into the old, pale green wallpaper.

Prepare for the coming of the King. He awaits His Watchman. He shall punish the unfaithful. He shall feast upon His arrival. He awaits His Watchman.

"What the hell does it mean?" Anne asked, looking at Brian.

"Nothing good," Brian answered.

He hit pause on the film and stood up.

"Are you okay?" Anne asked.

"Yeah," Brian said. He looked out the window. The little girl with the stuffed dog stood a dozen yards away and watched him. He sighed.

"I just need some coffee," he said, turning away from the window. He walked to Ken's percolator and looked back at her. He smiled tiredly and asked, "Do you want a cup?"

CHAPTER 22

KEN, THE LIBRARY AT MIDDLEBURY, JUNE 22ND, 1976

In 1973, Ken had turned on his television set just in time to catch the end of a report on Vietnam. It showed a Huey gunship going down.

Ken had turned his television off and given it to Mike Pinkham on first shift. Ken didn't want to watch anyone die ever again, and he sure as hell didn't want to do it while sitting in front of the television. In July of the same year, he heard about the accident at Logan Airport in Boston when a Delta flight had crashed. Eighty-nine deaths. Everyone on board.

The maintenance guys got the radio.

Ken preferred his books.

He read fiction. Mostly what the librarian told him were the seminal works of American and British literature. Nancy knew what she was talking about, so he always ran his choices by her before he checked them out.

Ken stayed away from newspapers and magazines. He didn't care about the news. He didn't care about politics, either local or national. They were all the same. He couldn't escape it, of course. He saw headlines when he went into the stores for groceries. He overheard people on the few occasions when he ate at a restaurant or at the chow hall in the Sanitarium.

His parents avoided talking about the news with him. They kept it pretty basic. He and his father talked about his father's work at the sawmill. His mother liked to talk about her friends and their eligible daughters.

Ken listened politely to both. He could care less about his father's foreman Jean being a pain and how the man should be shipped back to Canada. And Ken really couldn't bring himself to be concerned with Sue Wetherbee's excellent homemaking skills.

Ken hadn't even been interested in women. For some reason his time at Middlebury had killed his libido.

He wasn't attracted to men. He wasn't attracted to anyone.

His mother needed to remain blissfully ignorant of that fact.

All of these thoughts rolled through his head, as they always did after he spent time with his parents. Sunday dinners weren't unpleasant, just routine.

Ken sighed as he climbed the stairs to go into Middlebury's library. The building was an elegant Edwardian, decorated with Eastlake carvings, furniture, and walls and walls of bookcases.

When he went into the main room, he found Nancy at her desk. She looked up and smiled at him.

"Good evening, Ken," Nancy said. "How was dinner?"

"The same," he answered, returning the older woman's smile.

She took her glasses off and set them down on her blotter. She tucked a stray strand of gray hair back behind her ear and said, "So, since Sue Wetherbee was last week, who is your mother trying to set you up with this week?"

"This week," Ken said, sitting down in a chair close to the desk, "she would like to see me ask out a young woman named Henrietta Bloch. Henrietta, from what my mother has told me, has just graduated from high school. She is brilliant with her nieces and nephews, and her family has seven children, including Henrietta. All of the girls have had strong, healthy children."

Nancy laughed and shook her head. "And what about work?"

"Work?" Ken grinned. "Well, let's see. She can run a Singer sewing machine, she won the bake off at the Lutheran Church this past winter, and she won several ribbons from the Contoocook Four-H club."

"And your mother is generally confused about why you're not asking her out?" Nancy asked.

Ken nodded.

"Is your father in on it too?"

"Just a little," Ken said. "We went into the workshop for a smoke and a drink, and he asked who I was seeing."

"Did you tell him you weren't seeing anyone?" Nancy said.

"No. I lied. I told him I was seeing a second shift nurse, and I told him there was no need for me to buy the cow when I got the milk for free."

Nancy laughed and then she put her glasses back on. "And that settled it with your father?"

"Just about," Ken chuckled. "He told me my mom really wanted grandchildren, which is why she's campaigning so hard."

"Understandable," Nancy said. "I had to bite my tongue when my son was still single. But, since you've finished with your weekly dinner, have you come for something new to read?"

"I have," Ken grinned. "I have. Tell me, do you know any good westerns?"

"I know several," Nancy said. She tapped a finger on her desk and then she said, "Have you read the book, *Shane?*"

"Wasn't that a movie with Alan Ladd?" he asked.

Nancy nodded. "Yes. They based it on a book, though."

Something crashed on the second floor, and Ken leaped out of the chair.

"Is anyone else here?" he asked.

"No."

"Call security," Ken said. He moved quickly to the stairs and then he ran up them. He took them two at a time and listened.

Another crash sounded.

Ken turned into the second floor and paused.

The building had been designed as a library. Each room then was separate, but large, and no doors hung in the doorways. Something skittered off to Ken's right, and he turned towards it.

A book, lying on its back, was moving across the hardwood floor by itself.

Another crash broke the library's natural stillness.

It came from the Dr. Le Grande Psychology Room. A large section filled with up to date case studies and reports as well as works by renowned psychologists.

Someone was ripping the room apart.

Books flew past the doorway, and several of them quickly scurried out as if on their own.

And perhaps they did.

Anything was possible at Middlebury.

Ken heard footsteps on the stairs, and he risked a glance back. Nancy was halfway up. An angry frown had settled onto her face.

"Who is it?" she asked.

Ken gave her a confused look.

"Who is it?" she repeated.

"I don't know," Ken said.

"Stay there, Kenneth," Nancy said, storming up the rest of the way. She passed by him angrily and stepped over the books, which scurried out of the way with all of the awkwardness of frightened birds.

Ken followed her into the room as a fourth bookcase leaned forward precariously before it crashed to the floor.

Nancy came to a stop just inside of the room. "All of them."

"What?" Ken asked, confused.

"It's all of them. Look at the books."

At least a dozen of the books fled out of the room. They slipped past Ken and Nancy to join the others in the hall.

"And do you smell the perfume?" Nancy asked him.

Ken was about to say no when he realized he did smell it. A sweet scent reminiscent of lilacs.

"Genevieve," Nancy murmured. She looked at Ken. "And Klaus. As well as all of the children."

Only two shelves remained upright, and one of them started to shake.

"Klaus!" Nancy snapped.

The bookcase stopped.

Nancy lifted her head up slightly, and her nostrils flared. She turned to the right.

Ken did the same, and he saw a large book suspended in mid-air.

"Genevieve," Nancy said firmly. "Put it down."

Ken watched, surprised as the book was slowly lowered to the floor.

"The rest of you stop," Nancy commanded.

The soft sound of books being pushed across wood ceased.

"Now," Nancy said. "Back to the third floor."

"Nancy," Ken said. "What the hell just happened?"

She turned and looked at him. "You've been here long enough to know about the dead?"

Ken nodded. They had never spoken of it before, but he had assumed she knew as well.

Although not so intimately.

"Will you help me with the books?" she asked. "I'll put them back in order tomorrow, but I'd like to get them up off the floor."

"Sure," Ken said. He stepped gingerly around the books scattered upon the hardwood. He took each tipped over bookcase in turn and set it back. At some point, each shelf system had been secured to the wall.

The dead had worked them free.

"You're wondering who they are?" Nancy asked as he started to pick up books alongside her.

"I was," he answered.

"Shortly after the First World War," Nancy said, "there was the flu epidemic. Do you know anything about it?"

"No," Ken said.

"The flu we have today is based on Spanish Influenza," Nancy said, "which killed millions of people worldwide. It came through to New Hampshire, too, of course. They believe it spread from Massachusetts, but it doesn't really matter where it came from or how it got here. What matters is it did."

"Hundreds of people became sick. And, of course, people became sick here at the Sanitarium. It swept through, and they attempted to isolate children who were infected by placing them in the library. Genevieve and Klaus were the oldest at sixteen each. Fifteen other children, ranging in age from nine to fourteen, were placed here. They all died."

"Damn," Ken said softly.

Nancy nodded.

"Are they always this wild?" he asked. "Or are they usually quiet when people are around?"

"They're usually quiet," Nancy said, straightening up and shelving several books. "I don't know why they were like this today."

Ken went to ask another question and stopped. He found his voice and said, "I think I know why."

"Why?" Nancy asked, looking over at him.

Ken pointed to the floor which she had just cleared off.

Words were scratched deep into the wood.

Send the watchman away. We do not want him here.

Nancy looked at him, a confused expression on her face. "Why?"

"I don't know, Nancy," he said with a shrug. He bent down, picked up a book and put it on the shelf. "But I'd sure like to read *Shane* if you can find it."

CHAPTER 23
TALKING WITH KEN

Brian and Anne had reviewed all of the recordings, both the audio and video.

Eleanor had been the only sight to see, and she had been enough for Brian.

Anne, however, was excited by it.

"Do you think we'll see more ghosts?" she asked him.

Brian nodded. "Yeah. There are plenty of them around. It's just a matter of documenting them for the purchaser."

"It was totally amazing to see the writing," she said, glancing at the dark laptop screen.

"I just hope she doesn't do anything more than write," Brian said with a sigh.

"Do they really interact?" she asked.

"They do more than interact, Anne," Brian said seriously. "They kill."

The statement curbed her enthusiasm.

"I forget about the killing," Anne said after a moment. "I don't know how I can, but I suppose there's still the thrill of contact."

"It is exciting," Brian said. "But don't forget there's also danger and risk involved."

From beyond the kitchen door came the sound of the shower.

"Ah," Brian said with a smile, "our host is up."

"Who is he again?" Anne asked.

"Ken Buckingham," Brian said. "He's a really good guy. And, basically, he's the reason this place hasn't gone straight to hell."

"And what does he do?"

"He's the third shift security guard."

"Damn," Anne said. "Third shift? This place is creepy enough in the daytime. How long has he been on third shift?"

"Since 1969," Brian replied.

Anne blinked several times before she said, "1969?"

Brian nodded.

She shook her head as if she couldn't quite wrap her head around the time frame.

"1969," she said again. "Forty-seven years."

Brian stifled a yawn and stretched. The desire to rest and sleep rushed over him and he fought it back. He had too much to do.

Brian stood up, stretched and walked to the window behind the sink. He looked out and saw three ghosts standing together a few feet away from the tree line. They watched him, two men and a woman. As Brian yawned again, a giant dog trotted out of the woods. It looked to be a black German shepherd, but Brian couldn't be sure.

The animal came to a stop beside the woman and sat down. It too turned its attention to Brian.

Brian swallowed uncomfortably.

"Anne," he said.

"Yeah?" she asked.

"Could you come here for a moment, please?"

"Um, sure," she answered. Her chair legs scraped across the floor as she got up. A moment later she stood beside him. Her arm brushed against his, and the smell of her filled his nose.

Brian tried to ignore it.

"Do you see it?" he asked.

"See what... oh, damn. That's a big dog," she said after a moment.

Brian nodded. Part of him was relieved she could see it. Part of him wasn't.

"See what?" Ken asked as he entered the kitchen.

Both Brian and Anne jumped a little at the man's entrance.

"Sorry," Ken said, chuckling. He finished straightening his sweater as he walked over to them.

"Oh," Ken said after a minute. "This isn't good. This isn't good at all."

"Why?" Anne asked, looking at the man.

"She hasn't come out of the woods in years," Ken explained. "Maybe fifteen years now."

Anne glanced out the window. "The dog doesn't look like it's over fifteen years old."

"She's older than fifteen," Ken said, taking down a mug and pouring himself a cup of coffee before sitting at the table. "Much, much older."

"Anne," Brian said as he walked over and joined Ken, "this is Ken Buckingham, our host. Ken, this is Anne. She'll be helping me with the investigation."

"A pleasure," Ken said, smiling.

"Same here," Anne said, returning the smile.

Ken stood up as she sat down and then returned to his seat.

"A gentleman," Anne said, her smile broadening.

"Thank you," Ken said with a short bow of his head. "Old habits. They have saved my life here more than once."

"Really?"

Ken nodded.

"Ken," Brian said, "how old is the dog?"

"Exactly?" Ken asked. "I can't tell you how old she is exactly. I can tell you when I first met her, though."

"When was it?" Anne asked.

"February fifteenth," Ken said. He took a drink of his coffee. "February fifteenth, 1970."

CHAPTER 24

KEN, FEBRUARY 15TH, 1970, BEFORE IKE'S DEATH

When Ken walked into the main office to punch in, he saw Gus still sitting at his desk. Ken took his time-card out of its slot, slipped it into the clock, and then he replaced it.

"Everything okay, Gus?" he asked.

Gus shook his head.

"What's going on?" Ken said, stepping into Gus' office.

"We'll wait a minute or two, okay?" Gus asked. "I need Ike here before I tell you guys what the problem is. Take a seat, Ken."

"Sure," Ken said. He sat down in the worn leather chair across from Gus as the man picked up a pack of Lucky Strikes and got himself a smoke.

Once he had the cigarette lit, Gus leaned back in the chair and exhaled a long stream of smoke towards the ceiling. "You know, Ken, I always said I wouldn't smoke."

"Why'd you start?" Ken asked.

"Okinawa," Gus said. "Some of the caves we cleared, well, you get half a dozen people who crawl in there and die. It doesn't smell too fine. Smoking helped keep my chow down."

Silence fell over them as they waited. A few of the other third shift guards punched in, said hello and wandered off. Ike showed up and hit the clock at five of eleven, his usual time.

"Come on in, Ike," Gus said. "Close the door behind you, please."

Ike did as he was asked and then he took a seat beside Ken.

"What's the word, Gus?" Ike asked.

"The Dog's back," Gus said.

"Jesus H. tap dancing Christ," Ike said with a groan. He closed his eyes and leaned his head against the wall.

"Yup," Gus agreed.

"What?" Ken asked, looking from Ike to Gus. "Who's the Dog?"

"Dog's not a who but a what," Gus said. "Big old black German Shepherd. Mean as hell. Dangerous, too."

"Does it come around a lot?" Ken asked.

"She does," Ike answered. "Too much for my liking."

"She's been around since nineteen twenty," Gus explained. "At least, the earliest record we have of her for certain is nineteen twenty. One of the doctors saw her. If he hadn't been able to get the resident away from the Dog, I don't think anyone would have believed him."

"Wait," Ken said, shaking his head. "Are you telling me this dog's been alive for almost sixty years?"

"Yes," Gus said. "Do you doubt it here, Ken? Do you doubt Middlebury might have a dog near on sixty years old?"

"No. No, I don't," Ken answered.

"Who saw her?" Ike asked.

"Alex did. He was taking a walk around the back of the maintenance facility when he caught sight of her," Gus answered.

"What time?" Ike said.

"Two forty-five," Gus said.

"Damn," Ike said with a sigh.

"Why?" Ken asked, looking from one man to the other. "Why 'damn'?"

"The Dog strikes twelve hours after she's been seen by security," Gus explained. "So it means we have less than three hours to figure out where she's going to hit."

"She tells us?" Ken asked.

"If you know where to look," Gus said.

"And Gus knows," Ike continued. "See, Gus has dealt with her a few times."

"Twice," Gus said, correcting Ike. "Just twice. And the residents died each time."

"So," Ken said. "Where are we going to look?"

"You two are going to start behind the maintenance facility," Gus said. "Look for her tracks. They'll be big. Bigger than any dog's you've ever seen. Don't backtrack the Dog, okay? She never comes from where she'll make the kill, but she does go towards it. When the tracks stop, you'll be in the right area."

"What do we do after they stop?" Ken asked.

"You keep an eye open. Your ears too. You know what Middlebury is supposed to sound like at night," Gus said.

"Anything else?" Ike asked.

Gus shook his head. "Do your best. She's difficult, though. I already called the wife. She knows I'm staying here tonight."

Ken heard the dismissal in Gus' voice and stood up. Ike did the same.

"Okay, Boss," Ike said. "We'll check in soon as we find something."

Gus nodded.

Ken followed Ike out of the office and through the building to the February cold. They both paused on the building's stairs to put on their hats and gloves. Ken buttoned his collar up to his throat, adjusted his scarf and said, "Shotguns?"

Ike shook his head. "Won't work, kid. Nothing works on her."

"What about the first doctor? The one in the twenties?" Ken asked.

"He used his hands," Ike replied. "Tried a pistol first, but no luck with it. He tried a stick and a shovel, but only his fists worked. He finally managed to pry the damned Dog's mouth open. Gus tried a rifle on it. Thirty odd six. Nothing. Not even a drop of blood. By the time he got it off of the resident the Dog had already crushed the guy's head."

"Great," Ken said, looking out over Middlebury.

"Yeah. You know about once a year we lose a resident. Eventually, we find most of them. Dead, of course. But we find them. Occasionally though we don't. The bodies never show up. We figure the Dog or something worse got them."

"Something worse than an immortal dog?" Ken asked, looking at the older man.

Ike chuckled. "I know. I know. Yeah, though. There is something worse. A lot of things, actually. Anyway, let's get a move on."

"Fair enough," Ken said.

They walked down the stairs and over to the guardhouse where they picked up some flashlights and a couple of handheld two-way radios.

Alex was in the guardhouse, and he looked exhausted. His paper was folded in half and lay neglected on the counter. He smiled tiredly at Ken and

Ike.

"You okay?" Ike asked.

Alex gave a slight nod. "Don't want to go home until it's all done. Burke's gone off to get some coffee for us and a sandwich for me. What are you two doing?"

"The boss has us going to pick up her trail," Ike said.

"You be careful," Alex said sternly, looking first at Ike and then at Ken. "Do you understand?"

Ken could only nod, and Ike did the same.

"I was with Gus the last time in fifty-two. She ignored us completely. Just focused on the resident," Alex said. His voice dropped slightly. "We would have been dead too if she'd wanted it."

"We'll be careful, Alex," Ken said.

"We will," Ike said. "We'll call in every half an hour to let you know how it's going."

"Good. Thanks," Alex said. "Be quick and be safe. Call if you see anything. Hear anything. Hell, you smell something you call me."

"Will do," Ken agreed. He and Ike left the guardhouse and turned on their radios as they started to walk towards the far right of the grounds. The maintenance building was off near the back, a short distance from the tree line. All of the roads and paths had been cleared, even the path which ran the entire perimeter of the populated part of the grounds. Paths and forestry roads ran through the woods, but they were left alone until spring.

And they didn't have to look in the forest, from what Ken gathered.

The Dog would hunt among the residents.

He and Ike walked in silence, the sound of their feet in the cold air seemed to echo loudly off of the buildings. When they reached the short, squat maintenance building, only the exterior light was on. The men had punched out and left earlier. Clint, the second shift supervisor, lived on the campus and could respond to any emergency which might occur during third. Ken felt the urge to call the man in and have him ready to help.

He wanted everyone to be ready to help.

But it wasn't practical.

There were still plenty of employees who felt Middlebury was strange, but not haunted. People who believed the curious occurrences were the natural result of having so many mentally disturbed individuals in one place.

Those were mostly first-shifters, though. People who couldn't imagine anything extraordinary being attached to the sounds or sights or shapes they saw. Second-shifters had a better understanding of how the Sanitarium worked but no one understood it as well as the third-shifters did.

Third shift either made a man or broke him.

The third shift was all volunteers. A few had been sent to third as punishment, but then they had decided to stay when they understood the danger facing the residents. These unfortunate people didn't have to really fear the doctors or staff, although occasionally untrustworthy folks had to be put down. No, they only had to worry about the dead.

And for someone who was already suffering from some sort of mental ailment, it was more than enough.

No, third shift was a special place. Third-shifters were a special group of people.

Ken felt all of them should have been told.

"There," Ike said, pointing and interrupting Ken's train of thought.

Ken followed the line of Ike's finger and saw giant paw prints in the snow.

The tracks started immediately as if the Dog had materialized out of nothingness.

Perhaps it had, Ken thought.

He and Ike passed through the snow to the thin, cleared trail. The Dog's prints ran alongside it. Towards the crematorium and the boneyard. They turned on their flashlights and played the beams over the tracks. Silently Ken and Ike followed them, past the cemetery and its gates and its headstones. Past the dark and cold incinerator. The prints and tracks continued.

Soon they were far from the buildings and the air grew colder. Snow started to fall, and an unnatural stillness settled over the Sanitarium.

A figure appeared on the trail ahead.

It looked to be a woman.

The person stood with her back to them, and they slowed their pace down.

"Hello," Ike said, his voice coming out surprisingly gentle.

The woman turned around.

She wore a flannel robe and light pink pajamas. Her feet were clad in house-slippers, her brown hair clipped short. Her face was free of makeup, and she looked at them with a bemused smile.

Ken saw the snow build up on her shoulders and head and face. When she smiled, the snow fell to her breast.

"She's dead," Ken said softly to Ike.

"Yes," Ike said with a sigh. Louder, he said to the woman, "Do you need any help?"

"No," the woman replied, her voice sounding as if she was speaking underwater.

"Are you out for a walk?" Ken asked her.

"Yes," she said, smiling at him. "Yes I am, Kenneth."

His name on her lips sent a cold chill along his spine.

"The Dog is here," she said, looking at the dog's tracks which ran along the trail. The woman smiled at Ike. "She's come for her pound of flesh."

"Do you know where she's taking it from?" Ike asked.

"Yes."

"Will you tell us?" he said.

"No," the woman answered.

Ken's shoulders slumped.

"I'll take you there, though," she said. "Yes. The King requests I do."

Ike stiffened. "The King?"

"The King." She nodded happily. "Septimus Rex."

She turned and started along the path. She stayed a dozen yards ahead of them, and Ken and Ike let her keep the distance.

For another ten minutes they walked. Each step carried them farther from the last of the lit buildings.

"Oh Christ, look, Ken," Ike said, pointing with his flashlight.

At the far edge of the field, a man ran through the snow. Laughter, short and sweet and mad, rolled back to them.

The dead woman vanished.

The Dog appeared out of the shadows.

She was huge. A massive, black German Shepherd the size of a pony. She seemed to fly along the snow, kicking it up behind her with each thrust of her legs.

The man glanced back, saw her, and laughed harder as he ran.

Ken and Ike started to race towards the man. The unknown resident aimed himself at the forest, caught sight of Ken and Ike, and he laughed cheerfully.

His gleeful joy rang out even as the Dog struck him in the small of the back and sent him sprawling across the trail.

Ken could hear the man giggle over the Dog's snarls. Ken heard the man over the sound of the man's stomach being torn open.

Ike reached the pair half a step ahead of Ken and received a blow to his stomach from the Dog's blood covered muzzle. Ike doubled over and vomited. Steam rose up from the bile as he collapsed onto his side and the flashlight shattered as it hit the frozen earth.

Ken dropped his own light and threw himself onto the Dog even as she buried her muzzle back into the pit of the man's stomach.

"What a good dog!" the man said, tears of joy soaking his cheeks. "Do you see her? Do you see what a good dog she is?"

Ken ignored the man as he wrapped his arms around the Dog's massive neck and started to squeeze. Her rough hair dug sharply into his face, and the man started to punch Ken's forearms wildly.

"Leave her alone!" the resident shrieked. "She's a good dog! Leave her be!"

The Dog tried to shake Ken free, but he squeezed harder. She howled angrily as she pulled her face out of the man's guts. Innards and offal trailed from her teeth and her eyes rolled in their sockets as she tried to see Ken.

She took a few steps back and collapsed to her side. Ken bit back a scream of pain as his leg was slammed between her massive side and the snow covered earth. She sought to crush him under her weight, but Ken shifted his grip. Blood and drool splashed down on him, her breath fetid.

And Ike was there. He tried to help the resident, but the man threw a wild punch and connected with Ike's nose. Blood exploded down Ike's lips, and he glared down at the resident. He turned away from the dying madman to help Ken. But the wounded man grabbed a hold of his legs and pulled him down.

Ken's arms started to ache.

Christ, he thought desperately, *I can't let go.*

The Dog seemed to understand the situation perfectly, and she rolled.

Ken buried his face into her neck and held on even as the air was knocked out of him. His bones groaned, and his arms ached, snow packed down around his neck and was so cold it felt as though his flesh had been set aflame.

When the Dog came back to her feet, though, Ken still clung to her.

The resident let out a laugh which ended in a brutal choke. Ike got free of the man's bloody grip, and the Dog relaxed and sat down.

The madman was dead.

The Dog sat patiently and waited for Ken to let go.

He did so carefully. He eased away from her and stepped towards Ike. The Dog blinked as she looked from Ike to Ken. Her right ear twitched, and her nostrils flared. Her tail thumped the packed snow for a moment, and her ears perked up.

She tilted her head back to look up at the sky and let out a long, drawn out howl before she got on all fours. She looked at them once and then trotted off into the forest.

Ken looked at Ike and Ike looked at Ken.

"Ken," Ike said in a low, confused voice, "I think the Dog just howled your name."

Ken looked at where the Dog had gone and nodded.

The Dog had indeed howled, *Kenneth*.

CHAPTER 25

DIFFICULTY LISTENING

Anne couldn't stop herself.

She loved to listen to Brian speak. His voice was deep and strong, powerfully masculine in a way she never thought she would find attractive.

She liked the more feminine men. Slim builds. Scholarly. Men who cared about what they ate and how they dressed. Men who cared about the environment. Men her own age.

Single men.

Anne never fell for a married man. And even if she did, it wouldn't be for a forty-year-old who looked like he could out drink and out smoke a frat house on any big ten campus.

She was falling for Brian, though.

Falling hard.

He even smells good, she thought as they sat at the dining table in Ken's house.

No man smells good.

Brian did, though. Even when he was drinking coffee with whiskey in it at five in the evening. Brian smelled like a man ought to smell.

And Anne found she liked it.

A lot.

She felt terrible about it, too.

Brian's wife Jenny was a nice woman. Anne was all about women being united. All about females standing together and not trying to find out how another woman's husband might feel like in the dark.

Okay, girl, she told herself. *You need to rein these hormones in.*

It was hard, though.

She had seen the way Brian looked at her. The way he tried *not* to look at her.

He was attracted to her.

And he was trying not to be.

The hours they had spent together during the day had been phenomenal, though. All the trashy, steamy romance novels she had read in junior high school flashed before her eyes. She pushed the unrealistic scenes back into the locked rooms of her preteen years and tried to focus on Ken.

Because even after the disturbing story about the giant, black German Shepherd she only wanted to see how well Brian kissed.

"So you're ready for the library?" Ken asked.

"Yes," Brian said. "I'd love to get it wrapped up today and be out of here tomorrow. I hope you're not offended Ken."

Ken chuckled and shook his head. "Not at all, Brian. I'm impressed you're sticking it out. Most folks wouldn't. Especially not after yesterday."

"And this morning," Brian said with a sigh.

"What about this morning?" Ken asked.

Brian told them both about a little girl with a stuffed animal.

She had walked with Brian to Anne's car, but Anne had never seen her.

When he finished, Ken asked, "Was it a black and white terrier, the toy?"

"Yeah," Brian said. "You know her?"

"Yes," Ken said. "I don't know her name, though. I know the toy's."

"The toy has a name?" Anne asked.

"Oh yes," Ken said with a small smile. "Don't all the best toys have a name when you're a child?"

Anne smiled. "Yes. Yes, I guess they do. What's the dog's name?"

"Kenneth," Ken said grimly. "The dog's name is Kenneth."

CHAPTER 26

THE LIBRARY

The library was large, quiet, and full of books.

It was also warm.

Brian looked to Ken as the older man closed the door behind Anne.

"Hey, Ken," Brian said.

"Yes?"

"Why's it so warm in here?" Brian asked.

Ken smiled. "They don't like the cold."

"Who?" Anne asked.

"The dead in this building," Ken said, putting the hard-case he had carried up to a desk. "And since I'm not particularly fond of the cold either, I had a friend rig up a solar kit to help generate heat. I have absolutely no idea how it works, but it does."

"No complaints here," Brian said with a grin. He set the hard-case he carried beside Ken's. Anne came and did the same. She gently brushed his arm as she passed by and Brian felt a flutter of excitement in the pit of his stomach.

What the hell? Am I back in high school? he asked himself. He took a deep breath and said, "Ken, is there a place you recommend we put any recorders?"

"Second floor, the Dr. Le Grande Psychology Room," Ken said. "I would bring you up, but my mere presence antagonizes them. I usually come in, spend a few minutes finding a couple of books and leave. Are you both staying here tonight?"

"Yes," Brian said, glancing over at Anne, who nodded. "That would probably be best unless the residents here are like Eleanor?"

"No," Ken chuckled. "They get irritated, but they're nothing like Eleanor."

"Good," Brian said, feeling himself relax. "Great, actually."

"Well," Ken said. "I'll leave you to your work. I'll check on you when I do my rounds."

"Sounds great, Ken. Thanks again," Brian said.

"You're welcome. I'll see you both a little later on."

The older man left the library and closed the door tightly behind him.

"So," Anne said, smiling at him. "Second floor?"

"Sounds good to me," Brian said. "Let's get the gear out."

Together they opened the cases and removed the different video and audio recorders. They took out the power packs and wires, the laptops and boosters. They each took a pair of audio and video recorders and carried them up the main stairwell as they ran a bundle of cables up as well. The last of the evening light came in through tall windows and reminded Brian he needed to get the flashlights out.

The Dr. Le Grande Psychology Room was fair sized with a reading table against the far wall and between a pair of tall windows.

"This room's really clean," Anne said as they deposited the gear on the table.

"What do you mean?" Brian asked, looking around.

"No dust," she said, laughing.

The sound filled the room and sent a thrill through him.

"Oh," he said, grinning. "Yeah. I wonder if Ken dusts the place."

"Probably," Anne said. "His house is spotless. I'm impressed. A lot of people just don't take care of their homes with so much dedication."

"He's a special kind of man," Brian said, turning on the recorders. He positioned them on various shelves while Anne connected the power packs to them. In a few minutes, the room was ready to record.

Brian took a step back into the room's center and said, "Testing. Testing one, two, three. This is an audio and visual."

"All set?" Anne asked after he had stopped.

"Yeah," he said with a nod. "Let's go downstairs and make sure everything's running through like it should."

He led the way down to the first floor. They looked around for a few minutes and finally found a pair of chairs in a closed office. He and Anne dragged the chairs out to the desk and finished the equipment check and set up. They worked in silence for nearly half an hour and then Brian sat back in his chair.

He took his phone out to send Jenny a text and saw he didn't have any reception.

"Anne," he said.

"Yes?" she asked, looking up from the laptop.

"Do you have any reception on your phone?" he said.

She took her phone out of a pocket, unlocked it and frowned. She looked up at him. "No, nothing at all."

"Me neither." He put his phone away and tapped his fingers on the desk.

It's possible the snow from yesterday knocked out some towers somewhere, he thought. But his phone had worked after the storm when Anne had called him to see where he was.

Someone or something had decided to interfere with the phone.

Great.

Brian dug into his small gear bag, took out a small camping light and a Thermos of coffee along with a pair of paper cups. The coffee and cups had been provided by Ken. The light, a last minute addition when Brian had packed the equipment.

Brian turned the light on and set it on the desk. He put the Thermos and cups beside it.

"What do you think about the dog story?" Anne asked. She took off her gloves and put them on the floor next to her chair. She removed her hat and coat as well. Brian watched, fascinated as she ran her fingers through her hair.

"Um, the dog story?" he managed after a moment. "Well, I think it's true."

"Really?" Anne asked. "A dog almost sixty years old?"

Brian smiled at her. She had only seen Eleanor's hand and the writing on the wall.

"This place is strange," Brian said, the smile fading away. "Yesterday was rough. A lot of the dead showed up. The only evidence I captured, however, was Eleanor. I think the recording of her could easily be argued against, though."

"Really?" she asked, surprised.

Brian nodded. "I'm certain someone would say we had help or a good editing program. Something. I don't know if the State wants this sale to go through, or if the buyer really wants to buy it. Who knows? But I want to do the job right."

"Fair enough," Anne said, smiling. "So, think you could pour me a cup of coffee?"

"Sure," Brian said, chuckling. He opened the Thermos and poured out some of the dark brew into each cup. Steam curled up, and the smell of the hot liquid was sublime. Brian handed her drink to her and settled back to enjoy his own. After a few moments, he asked, "What were you doing before this for work?"

"I was working in an antique store. High-end place," Anne answered. "Out in Milford. I'm still trying to decide if I want to continue on with a master's program or get a full-time job."

"What would you study?" Brian asked.

"Psychology," she said. "I'd like to be a therapist, but I'm not one hundred percent certain. And if I'm not completely sure, then I don't want to waste the time or money, you know?"

Brian nodded. "I do."

He started to take another drink and stopped.

Behind Anne, at the edge of the camping light's reach, a child stood in the shadow and watched them.

"What's wrong?" Anne asked softly.

"There's a child here," Brian answered. "Don't turn around."

"You can see it?" Anne whispered.

Brian nodded. "Do me a favor. The camera next to you on the desk, reach over slowly and turn it on."

Anne did so.

Brian stretched out slightly, keyed the laptop and brought up the camera Anne had just powered up. When the video feed was live, Brian turned the computer to face Anne.

"Do you see the child?" he asked her softly.

"No," she answered after a moment. "I don't see anything. You do?"

"Yes," Brian said. He looked at Anne. "I think it's a little boy. Maybe ten or so. He's just watching us."

"How can you see him?" Anne asked. "Is the camera not picking him up?"

"The camera is," Brian said. "Or I can still see him through the camera."

"How?" Anne said. "How can you see him and I can't?"

"I hit my head yesterday," Brian said after a moment. "And ever since, I've seen the dead."

CHAPTER 27

IAN AT MIDDLEBURY

Since the end of August, Ian Harris had waited and watched.

Middlebury Sanitarium was his next target. He needed to get in and get a good look at the architecture of some of the smaller buildings. A few of the urban spelunking sites had showed some excellent mantels and built-ins, but Ian specialized in ceiling medallions and light fixtures.

And right before August rolled into September, someone had posted pictures of a house in Middlebury Sanitarium. For over a week Ian had researched the place and was finally able to identify the house.

It was at the back of the center of the campus, near the cemetery. The head nurse's house.

Ian needed to get the rhythm of the place. And, quite frankly, he had other houses and buildings to work through as well. Ian did more than well for himself selling items via the Darknet. No messy middle-men, no investigators who poked their noses into the indoor flea markets.

No, Ian was a choirboy compared to some of the crimes committed through the anonymity of the Darknet. The local, state and federal cops had a lot more to worry about than Ian moving stolen architectural pieces.

And everything was paid for in Bitcoin, mailed out courtesy of the USPS to anonymous post office boxes.

Plus, and here was the best part, Ian was able to enjoy the thrill of the hunt. He loved to track the movements of the rent-a-cops, plan ways into and out of the buildings. The thrill he had felt as a child when he would dress all in black and sneak into neighbors' houses to see what they had in their basements or attics.

He was able to enjoy the same thrill when sneaking into an abandoned house. Especially in a place under watch.

Or, Ian chuckled, *theoretically under watch.*

He wasn't sure exactly how much the old, third shift security guard actually saw. The man usually smoked and read between hourly strolls around the sanitarium.

Ian had caught sight of another man watching the place, but he recognized him as a spelunker. The man didn't even know the right way to get around the place.

But Ian did.

Ian knew about the tunnels. He would be able to move from house to house once he was in.

He smiled to himself and took his backpack off of the passenger seat of his non-descript, blue Toyota Camry. He quickly double checked his equipment. A lock-pick set, headlamp with a red lens, a Dremel tool adjusted to run on a battery, and a small screwdriver set.

Everything he needed to strip out his next month's salary from the house.

And if the guard stayed out of the houses, Ian could press his luck and slip into the other houses as well. Middlebury Sanitarium could prove to be a goldmine.

Ian needed to be patient. He needed to move carefully. He hadn't reached the age of thirty as a professional thief, without having done any jail time, by being careless.

Caution was the watchword as far as Ian was concerned.

Ian took a deep breath, let it out slowly, and then he zipped the backpack closed and got out of the car. He put the pack on, shut the door gently, and started down the road. He kept close to the brick wall which surrounded the Sanitarium, saw the spot where the boughs of an evergreen hung low and heavy with snow, and slipped over the wall.

Ian hunkered down in the snow and watched the guardhouse.

The old man stepped out of the small building, stretched, and then walked away. Pipe smoke curled up and trailed behind the man and Ian smiled. Ian waited patiently until the guard was no longer visible.

Ian stood up quietly and moved quickly through the snow. He knew exactly where the head nurse's house was. He had his bearings and felt comfortable in the bright light of the full moon. Ian had nothing to worry about. He needed only to get to the house, to get inside, to get what he could carry, and get back to the car.

The snow from the previous storm covered the ground. The snow was light and easy to walk through. Ian wanted to whistle but knew he couldn't.

The sound would carry too far.

Within a few minutes, he saw the house. He recognized it from the images he had studied during the preparation phase.

He knew there was a backdoor, and he moved to the left of the building toward it. The cemetery was to his left, and the land was quiet.

Far quieter than it should be.

The tracks of some large animal also cut between the cemetery and the house, and the prints were fresh. Ian had never hunted, had never wanted to spend so much time in the woods, no matter how often his father and uncles had tried to get him to.

Ian pushed the thoughts away as he rounded the corner of the house. The backdoor was there, exactly where it was supposed to be, and Ian hurried to it. He took hold of the knob, twisted carefully and was pleasantly surprised to find it unlocked.

He grinned as he opened the door and slipped into the building. He paused, shed his backpack and took out his headlamp and his tools. The sconces on either side of the door were stunning, and Ian sighed happily.

Twenty minutes. Twenty minutes tops, he told himself. He would be able to get a good supply of items within fifteen, and then another five to tidy up.

Ian straightened up.

Something had scratched at the pantry door.

He looked at the door, the red of his light illuminated it and the cut-glass doorknob.

I should take it, too, he told himself.

The knob turned to the left, and then to the right. Ever so slowly it continued, back and forth. Ian watched it, both horrified and fascinated.

Finally, the knob moved far enough to the left, and a soft 'click' sounded.

The door opened and swung in a wide arc. It came to a stop right before the wall, and the darkness beyond swallowed the red light and beckoned him forward.

Ian raised a foot and then he forced it back to the floor.

Run, a voice said urgently. *Run.*

He couldn't.

He had to see what was in the pantry.

"Do you like dogs?" a woman asked. "I like dogs. Do you like dogs?"

Ian nodded, and the beam of his light bobbed up and down.

"We're so glad," the woman said happily.

And the largest dog Ian had ever seen launched itself out of the pantry.

He was knocked backward and slid across the floor, the dog on top of him. He could smell its breath as the dog opened its mouth and bit down on either side of his face.

Ian screamed.

CHAPTER 28
A SILENCE BROKEN

Ken was halfway to the library when he heard the scream.

It came from behind.

Ken turned around and headed back towards the center of the campus. He paused every few steps and listened, yet nothing sounded off again. When he reached the guardhouse, he came to a stop and stared.

The lights were on at Isabella's.

The door was open.

His heart started to beat rapidly and his mouth dried out.

Ken hadn't seen her in decades.

The door was open.

He had no choice.

With his head slightly bent, Ken walked toward Isabella's house.

CHAPTER 29

THE CHILDREN

Brian watched the child, and the child watched Brian. Soon a second little boy joined the first and Brian noticed they were twins. Fair haired and dressed in nightshirts. They looked at him with a mixture of curiosity and anger.

Anne still had her back to them, and Brian could see she was uncomfortable.

"Are they still there?" she asked, her voice low.

"Yes," Brian answered.

"What are they doing?"

"Just watching me," he said.

A third child appeared. A girl who was taller and thinner than the other two boys. Her skin was slightly darker, her brown hair pulled back and tied off with a ribbon of blue. She too wore a nightshirt.

The smell of lilacs drifted through the room, and something rattled on the second floor.

Anne leaned forward and clicked the laptop's mouse.

The screen divided itself into four. Three of the four blocks showed the Dr. Le Grande Psychology Room while the fourth remained focused on the area behind Anne. In the new images books slowly migrated off of the shelves one at a time to fall onto the floor.

A child's laughter rang out, and footsteps raced along the upper hall.

Anne stiffened. "I heard someone."

Brian smiled. "You did. More than one."

Someone was behind the shelves upstairs. Brian caught a glimpse of black hair behind the books.

"How many are there now?" Anne asked.

"At least one upstairs in the room, probably another in the hall. Three, no four down here," Brian said as another girl, slightly older than the twins but younger than the first girl appeared.

"Damn."

Brian nodded.

The older girl stepped forward into the light. She looked at Brian. Then she walked a little closer.

"You see us," the girl said.

"I do," Brian answered.

Anne looked at him, a confused expression on her face. He shook his head slightly, and she remained quiet.

"Does the lady?" the girl asked.

Brian shook his head.

"You know Ken?" the girl said.

Brian took a deep breath and answered, "I do."

The girl frowned. "I don't like Ken. None of us like Ken."

"Why?"

"Because the King likes him," the girl said sharply. "And because *she* likes him."

"Who's the King?" Brian asked. "Who is 'she'?"

"She is Isabella," the girl said angrily. "Foul, wretched woman. Eater of the dead. And He, well, He is Septimus Rex. The King of Middlebury Sanitarium. King of the Dead. Let us hope you never meet Him."

"It sounds more and more like I really don't want to," Brian said.

"You have to leave," the girl said.

"I will, soon," Brian said.

"No," the girl said fiercely. "You have to leave. He's coming. He doesn't want you here."

"Who?" Brian asked.

"The King," she said, spitting out the title. "He is coming, and Hell's coming with Him."

"Brian," Anne said softly, "did it just get really cold in here?"

Brian was about to answer 'no' when he realized it had.

It was terribly cold. His breath suddenly exploded into a stream of white as it exited his mouth.

The girl stepped back and looked nervously around her. The other children vanished. Somewhere a window shattered.

"Get out," the girl hissed. "Get out now."

Brian stood up, and Anne did the same a heartbeat later.

"What's wrong?" Anne asked. "What's going on?"

"I don't know," Brian said. More windows broke in the library. "But they want us to leave."

"The kids?" Anne asked, pulling on her coat and snatching up her gloves and hat.

"Yup," he said. He glanced up, but the girl was gone, too.

Beyond the library's walls, the wind suddenly picked up. It battered the building and screamed with an ungodly rage.

A book hurtled down the stairs flew across the floor and struck Brian full in the face. He staggered, fell, and then sprawled out on the floor.

"Take it!" someone shrieked.

Anne snatched up the book and offered her hand to Brian. With his head fuzzy and pulsing Brian took her hand and got to his feet.

Hand in hand, they ran for the door.

CHAPTER 30
AN UNWANTED INTERVIEW

Ken walked into Isabella's house and felt his stomach twist nervously.

The door clicked shut behind him, and he found himself once more in the parlor.

A small fire burned cheerfully in the hearth and an oil lamp's flame flickered by the grand chair Isabella sat in.

She wore the same dress he had seen upon her all those decades before, and she flashed him a smile of the same, deadly teeth. She held a piece of needlework in a hoop in her hands and set it down on her lap. From the table at her side, she lifted a glass goblet filled with a dark fluid and sipped from it. When she returned it to its place, her lips were a dark red.

From her sleeve, she drew forth a lace handkerchief, dabbed delicately at her mouth, and then she tucked it away again.

"Kenneth," she said happily. "What a pleasure. Will you sit?"

"Of course, Isabella," he said politely. He removed his hat and sat in the chair across from her. He felt much as he had the first time they had met.

"You've been having a rather exciting time these past few days," she said with a wicked smile.

"A little too exciting," Ken said.

She laughed pleasantly. "Very true. The King has returned."

Ken could only nod.

"It is a thrilling moment in history, Kenneth," she said confidentially. "He is so looking forward to this time. Do you know this?"

"Yes, Isabella," Ken said, trying to repress a shiver.

"Oh Kenneth," she said with a sigh. "You need fear nothing. He is pleased with you. Your loyalty these long years. He shall reward you."

Ken felt cold at the mere thought of seeing the King again let alone receiving a reward of some sort.

"Who are these guests of ours, Kenneth?" Isabella asked in a soft voice.

"People hired to see if the Sanitarium is haunted," Ken replied.

"How curious," Isabella said. "Do they not trust the men whom they have hired to guard this place?"

Ken shook his head.

Isabella frowned. "This shall not please the King."

Ken swallowed nervously.

"Where are they now?" Isabella asked, her voice growing stern.

"In the library," Ken answered.

"With the children?" she said. "Was your decision a wise one, Kenneth?"

"Yes," Ken said, looking at her. "The children dislike me. They don't care about others."

"Ah, yes," Isabella said as she nodded. "I had forgotten their particular feud with you. Why is it so?"

"Because I am the King's Watchman."

"Yes," Isabella whispered, "you are."

Someone groaned in the basement, and Ken jumped.

Isabella chuckled and asked, "Did you forget they were there, Kenneth?"

He nodded.

"Well, dear Kenneth, they are still there. Quiet of late. Do you know why?"

Ken was afraid to ask, but he felt as though he had to.

"Why, Isabella?"

"The rats," she said, smiling. "I've added more rats. Mostly to eat their lips and teeth. As enjoyable as screams and howls and gibberish can be, there are moments when even I tire of it."

"Oh."

Isabella tilted her head slightly. "I think, my dear Kenneth, something is taking place outside."

"Yes," Ken said, happy for the distraction. "I thought I heard something a little while ago."

"The scream?" she asked.

"Yes."

She shook her head. "You needn't worry about it. Some thief. Eleanor introduced him to the Dog."

Ken fought to control the bile which rose in his throat.

"No," Isabella continued, "I mean the sound of glass breaking. I think it's coming from the library."

Ken stiffened, but he didn't rise up from the chair.

Isabella looked at him and then clapped her hands together happily. "You are such a delight, Kenneth! Go. Go to our guests and see what it is which has disrupted the silence of our home."

Ken stood up and bowed to her. "Thank you, Isabella."

"Thank you, Kenneth," she said with a sigh as she took up her needlepoint. "It's a shame the King has marked you for His own. I would have loved to have had you with me these long years."

"Thank you, Isabella," Ken replied. Behind him, the door opened, and he turned and hurried to it.

CHAPTER 31

RUNNING

Brian got to the street, realized he still had Anne's hand in his own and let go of it.

She blushed and quickly put on her gloves before she handed him the book which had hit him.

"Thanks," Brian said. Before he could look at the title, the wind slammed into them both and forced them back down the road half a dozen steps.

"What's happening?" Anne asked, looking around.

"The King is coming," Brian said.

"Brian! Anne!"

Brian turned and saw Ken. The older man hurried towards them. His flashlight bobbed and the moon shined brightly upon them.

"Are you okay?" Ken asked as Brian and Anne went to him.

"I think so," Brian said as Anne nodded.

"What happened to your face?" Ken said. "You look like someone punched you in the eye."

Brian frowned and held up the book. "I got hit with this. Someone threw it at me and told me to take it."

"Well," Ken said, "you better listen. I'll bring you to my place, and you two can hunker down there. Plenty of canned goods if you don't mind heating them up. Usually, I head into town and grab a meal, but not tonight. I've got to go to the head nurse's house."

"What happened?" Brian asked as they all started to walk towards Ken's house.

"Eleanor and the Dog," Ken said.

"How bad is it?" Anne asked.

"Don't know yet," Ken answered.

"How do you know it was Eleanor and the dog then?" she said.

"Isabella told me," he said. "They're all getting ready."

"Who?" Anne said.

"The dead," Brian said.

Ken nodded.

"They're not here," Brian said, looking around. "I don't see any of them."

"They're gathering some place. Some place close," Ken said, and Brian could hear the nervousness in the man's voice. "I'd love to get you two out right now, but I have to check the head nurse's house. I need to get the Dog away if she's there."

"She's not there," Anne said.

"What?" Ken asked.

Anne came to a stop, her face a deathly white.

Brian and Ken stopped beside her, and Brian followed her line of vision.

She stared at Ken's place and the Dog, who sat patiently on the front step.

And when Brian looked at it, the Dog started to growl.

CHAPTER 32
INTO HIDING

Brian knew he couldn't outrun the Dog.

No one could.

"Brian, Anne," Ken said in a calm voice. "Do you see the small building off to your left?"

Brian glanced and saw a narrow brick shed. The number '7' was painted on the lintel.

"Yes," Brian said.

"Yeah," Anne replied.

"Well," Ken said, "we're all going to walk towards the building. If the Dog comes off the stairs, make for the door. It's unlocked."

"What about you?" Anne asked.

Ken gave a tired chuckle. "I'll slow the Dog down."

"Okay," Brian said, holding onto the book tightly. "Let's go."

The Dog watched them.

Half a dozen feet from the shed the Dog leaped off of the stairs.

The three of them ran for the door. Anne reached it first and opened it so forcefully the door bounced off the wall. Ken's flashlight danced crazily around the walls as he pulled the door closed.

A second later, the door shuddered loudly as the Dog slammed into it.

Ken pointed his flashlight at a small, narrow door set into the far brick wall.

"Open it," he said, and Brian did so.

A set of stairs led down to a cement floor. A pair of heavy-duty, older model flashlights hung from carrying straps just inside of the doorframe.

"Each of you take a light," Ken said, raising his voice over the sound of the Dog and cracking wood.

Brian and Anne hurriedly did so, and Ken gestured to the stairs.

"Down we go," he said.

Brian turned on his flashlight. The beam wide and powerful. Anne did the same, and she followed him as he descended to the sub-level. Once more Ken brought up the rear. He closed and locked the door behind them, and when he reached the floor, they all heard the door to the shed shatter beneath the weight of the Dog.

The snuffling and sniffing of the Dog raised the hackles on Brian's neck, and the anxious whine she let out made his heart pound.

Ken slipped past them and then he turned around.

"These are the tunnels under Middlebury," he said, a tight, concerned look on his face. "They connect all of the buildings to one another. Some tunnels lead off into unknown places. There are seven buildings like the one we came through. Emergency exits to the grounds. Once a year I have to patrol through the tunnels, usually with two other guards.

Ken paused. "There are things down here that are not...particularly fond of people. Stay close to me. None of the doors you find will be locked, but unless I open it, don't touch it. Middlebury doesn't allow the doors to be locked down here. Do you understand?"

Brian nodded.

"This is about the only place left in the world that still scares the Hell out of me." Ken said.

"Middlebury doesn't let the doors be locked?" Anne asked. "Don't you mean the State of New Hampshire doesn't?"

"No," Ken said grimly, "I mean the Sanitarium. It doesn't like the doors to be locked. I stopped trying a long time ago. So, just follow me. Don't stop unless I stop. Don't run unless I run. And beware of everything."

Ken looked at them for a moment longer, and then he turned and led the way into darkness.

CHAPTER 33

KEN GOES UNDER, JULY 1ST, 1977

When Ken punched in a little before eleven on Friday night, Gus was there at his desk. Ken glanced over at him uncomfortably.

Gus nodded. "It's never good when I'm here late, Ken."

"Yeah," Ken said, stepping into Gus' office. "I've noticed. What's going on?"

"Well," Gus said, leaning back in his chair and putting his hands behind his head. "You know how Lenny retired this year?"

"Yup."

"Since he retired," Gus said with a sigh, "I need another man for the inspection. A solid guy who won't break, and you're the only person who's not currently on the inspection team who fits the bill."

Ken frowned. "What inspection are you talking about, boss?"

"The tunnel inspection. It needs to be done."

"I thought no one uses the tunnels. Aren't they all secured?" Ken asked.

Gus shook his head. "Not by far. Ernie will be doing the inspection with us. He's at maintenance right now, getting some of their super-flashlights."

"I thought Ernie wasn't doing third anymore," Ken said. "Not since his wife got sick."

"He's not," Gus said. "He's getting a little bit of overtime and a whole hell of a lot of money to do this with us."

"It's going to be bad?" Ken asked after a moment.

"The potential for it to go straight to hell is right at the top," Gus said in a grim voice. "The tunnels are bad, Ken. Officially we stopped using them in nineteen fifty. There was a pretty bad accident in the tunnel connecting Building One to Building Two. To top it off we had a doctor, and a nurse disappear down there, too. But that was in forty-nine."

"What?" Ken asked, feeling confused. "How the hell can you disappear in the tunnels?"

"Some of the tunnels don't go anywhere, Ken," Gus said softly. "They aren't marked on the maps. Any of the maps. These tunnels look like the originals, but they just don't go anywhere. When we go in, we go together. We walk together. We stay together. If I can't touch you, you're too far away."

"If it's so bad, Gus," Ken said. "Why are we going in?"

"To make sure nothing is getting out," Gus said. "And to make certain none of our missing have ended up in there."

Ken started to ask another question, but Ernest came into the room. He was short and stocky, a miniature Atlas. He carried the three large flashlights, each of them nearly the size of a briefcase, in one hand. He nodded to Gus and Ken.

"How are you doing, Ken?" Ernie asked, extending his free hand.

"Doing well, Ernie," Ken said, shaking it. "How's your wife?"

Ernie shrugged. "She's a tough old bird. She's hanging in there. Don't know for how much longer, though."

"I'm sorry," Ken said.

Ernie nodded and turned to Gus. "We ready, boss?"

"About as ready as we'll ever be," Gus said, pushing his chair away from his desk and standing up. "Grab a flashlight, Ken. Let's get this done with."

Ken nodded, picked up one of the lights and waited for Gus to do the same and then to lead them on their way.

Gus left the office with Ken and Ernie trailing behind him. The older man walked swiftly to the stairwell and went into it. Gus flipped on his own flashlight and illuminated a dark shadow. A slim door was revealed and surprised Ken. He'd been through up and down the stairs before, and he'd never known about the door.

"Lights, gentlemen," Gus said, and Ken turned on his own flashlight a moment after Ernie. "Remember what I said, Ken. We stay within touching distance at all times."

"You got it, Gus," Ken said.

Gus nodded, took a deep breath, and opened the door.

The smell of stale air, tinged with ancient death, spilled out into the stairwell. Another set of stairs descended into darkness, and Ken felt his stomach tighten, and his testicles retract.

Jesus, Ken thought. *This is bad.*

But he followed Gus as the man went down the stairs. Ernie brought up the rear and closed the door behind them. A sense of hopelessness swept over Ken as the latch caught and clicked.

"Don't worry, Ken," Ernie said in a comforting tone. "Middlebury won't lock us in. She never locks any of us in."

"Always a first time," Gus said in a warning tone. "So keep awake."

"Sleeping is the last thing I would do down here, boss," Ken said.

The three men swept the beams of their flashlights over the walls, ceiling and floor. They walked upon a pale gray tile, the walls of smooth cement which rose to an arch a few feet above their heads. The hall was cold and dark sconces with frosted glass shades stood every thirty feet.

As the beams moved along ahead of them, Ken caught sight of a door set into the right wall. The number '27' was painted in bright white on the wood.

Ken glanced back at the door, but Ernie tapped him gently on the shoulder.

"Eyes front, chief," Ernie said lightly. "We don't worry about any closed doors."

"And there are never any open doors?" Ken asked, coming to a stop.

Gus and Ernie were both forced to stop. The older men frowned as they looked at him.

"Yeah, kid," Gus said, trying to keep the frustration out of his voice. "There aren't ever any open doors."

"Well, what about the one on the left?" Ken asked, and he pointed his beam at a door just at the edge of his light.

Gus and Ernie turned and brought their flashlights up to join his.

A door stood slightly ajar. The number 1949 was painted on the wood.

"What the hell?" Ernie asked.

"Stay on me," Gus said tightly. "Both of you."

The three of them formed a rough triangle. A half a step too far forward and Ken would walk into Gus. If he hesitated, Ernie would walk into him.

The room was bad.

He could feel his blood pound in his veins. He started to sweat despite the chill of the tunnel. Every sound became magnified.

Soon they were at the door, which swung wide at their approach.

Together they stopped at the threshold and Gus shined his light into the room beyond.

The same tile on the floor of the tunnel was carried into the room and up the walls.

"Do we go in?" Ernie asked.

Before Gus could answer Ken said, "Yes."

Gus glanced over his shoulder at him. "You sure, kid?"

Something told Ken 'yes,' and so he said, "Yeah, I'm sure."

"Okay," Gus whispered, and he stepped into the room.

The three of them moved quickly, and the room lengthened and widened as they walked in deeper.

"Gus," Ernie said.

"Yeah?"

"The door."

Ken looked behind him and saw the door was directly behind Ernie, even though they walked steadily away from it.

"Damn," Gus said. "Guess Middlebury doesn't want us getting lost in here."

"Guess not," Ernie agreed.

"Hello?" a voice asked out of the darkness.

It was a woman. Her voice came from far ahead of them.

"Holy—" Ernie whispered.

"Hello," Ken said, stepping in front of Gus and taking the lead.

Footsteps echoed. Slowly at first and then quicker. Gus forced himself to walk cautiously.

A moment later, a woman ran out of the darkness and into the light.

Her blonde hair was disheveled, her makeup smeared. Desperately she kept a bloodied doctor's coat clutched around her naked body. Her blue eyes dashed about wildly.

"My God," Gus whispered.

"Help me!" the woman sobbed. "Oh please, help me!"

Ken caught her in his arms and pulled her close. The blood was fresh, and the stink of iron filled his nose. She shook in his arms.

"Watchman," a small voice sang from the darkness beyond the

flashlights. "Watchman."

More voices joined the first until it sounded as though dozens of them called out.

"Who the hell is the watchman?" Ernie asked, a note of worry creeping into his voice.

"I am," Ken said. "I'm the watchman."

He gently passed the woman to Gus.

"Come hither, fair and loyal Watchman," the voices sang.

Ken took a step forward.

"Ken," Gus said.

Ken glanced back at him and smiled. His heart pounded against his chest as he said, "I have to, Gus. I'll be right back. Middlebury doesn't want me down here."

Before Gus could say anything else, Ken walked forward.

The beam of his own flashlight broke free of the others as he stepped further into the curious room. The voices continued to call for him. They remained soft and gentle, playful as they called to him.

After a few minutes, blood appeared on the floor. Just a few drops, then a pair of women's shoes, black kitten heels. Torn nylons. A ripped white skirt and a matching blouse. An antique nurse's cap on its side. Panties and a brassiere.

The blood thickened.

Men's Oxfords. Tweed pants and a pressed shirt. Boxer shorts and a t-shirt.

Blood was everywhere.

And then Ken reached the wall, the owners of the voices and the source of the blood.

Small, vile creatures of pale white, perhaps half a foot high. Skin stretched taut over thin bones. Milky white eyes and toothless mouths. They looked like perverted versions of sprites or fairies. Each finger on their small hands was tipped with a jagged black nail.

The strange little things crawled over and around a bloody form slumped against the wall. It had been a man, at one time, yet they had skinned him. They fed themselves, and each other bits of the skin, pulled at the muscles and toyed with the tendons.

And the man was still alive.

His wide, maddened eyes dashed about, robbed of their eyelids. His mouth, barren of the tongue, tried to scream, but his lips had been severed and devoured.

"Watchman," the things cried out as one. "Behold madness and lust in its purest form."

Ken turned and ran for the light of his friends.

Chapter 34
Seeking Shelter

"The Dog's not trying to get down here," Anne said.

"Of course not," Ken said. "The Dog's smarter than we are."

Brian felt uncomfortable. The tunnel was wrong. Paul Kenyon had been a choir boy compared to what waited under the earth and between the buildings. Brian could feel it in his gut. It was a strange feeling wishing he was facing that deranged little bast…"

"You okay, Brian?" Ken asked.

"Yeah," Brian said. "Quicker we're above ground the better, though."

"Truer words were never spoken," Ken said, leading the way.

"How long until we get to the next door?" Brian asked.

"The next door to another building?" Ken said.

"Yeah," Brian replied.

"Depends," Ken said.

"What do you mean?" Anne asked.

"I mean it all depends on Middlebury," Ken said. "Sometimes it might take a few minutes to walk from Building Two to Building One. The next year it might take three hours. It all depends."

"How is that even possible?" Anne asked. "It doesn't make any sense. It's not natural."

"I think you just answered the question," Brian said gently. He continued to follow Ken. Anne, in turn, stayed close to Brian. The powerful beams of the flashlights swept back and forth in front of them, and the tunnel continued.

Whispers slipped out of the shadows, fell upon them from the ceiling.

Brian knew they were far from alone.

Yet he hadn't seen any of them.

The dead hid from them. The dead hid from *him*.

Why? he thought. *Why are they hiding?*

"What are they saying?" Anne asked softly.

"You don't want to know," Ken said, his voice grim.

A pair of doors appeared on the left. One was numbered 1899, and the other 1919.

"How many doors are down here?" Brian asked.

"Too many," Ken said. They passed by the portals. "Those aren't their markers, though."

"What are they?" Anne asked.

"Years," Ken answered. "Those are the years those doors were made."

"What? You mean someone came in here and installed them?" Brian asked.

"No," Ken said. "Something terrible happened down here in those years."

The older man played his flashlight over another door, the beam illuminating a white '1949.' "Take this one for example."

"What about it?" Brian asked.

"When I first saw it, back in the seventies, it was open," Ken said. He paused and looked at the door.

"So this one was made in nineteen forty-nine?" Anne asked.

"Yeah," Ken said.

"What happened?" Brian asked. "Why did Middlebury put this door in?"

"Doctor and a nurse were walking from Building Four to Three. Bad snow storm. She was a pretty woman. He was a rotten man. He dragged her into an open room and had his way with her."

"What happened to him after?" Anne asked, anger in her voice as she stared at the door.

"After?" Ken asked.

"After they found out she was raped," Anne said, looking at him.

A hideous, wretched moan came through the door, and Brian took a nervous step back.

"He's still in there," Ken said, turning away from the door. "We found her in seventy-seven."

"She was still alive?" Anne asked, horrified.

"It had just happened, for all she knew," Ken said. "Time can be funny down here."

"What was done with her?" Brian asked.

"She went mad when we got her upstairs, and she saw the year. She didn't believe it. She ended up living in Building Three until nineteen eighty-two," Ken said. "Come on."

He started to walk again.

"Did she get better?" Anne asked.

"No," Ken said with a sigh. "The King killed her. Killed her along with all of the other people in three one night. Ah, look. There's a door."

Brian looked and saw a door marked, 'Building 2'.

Ken moved to it, grasped the steel doorknob, twisted, and opened it easily.

Stairs led up to a second door.

And the little girl with the stuffed dog stood at the top and looked down on them.

CHAPTER 35

THE GIRL WITH THE DOG, JUNE 6, 1989

Middlebury Sanitarium was a ghost town, both literally and figuratively.

The staff, other than Ken, no longer lived on the grounds. Of all the housing units, only Building Four was occupied, and not even completely.

A single trio of men served on first shift for security. Another set of three for second. Ken alone protected the remaining patients on third. The dead, however, still remained. The Factory still produced its ghosts.

Some of them Ken feared. Some of them he ignored. Others he avoided. When he could.

In the warm summer air, Ken walked slowly. He smoked his hunting pipe steadily and traveled along his regular route, one he hadn't altered in almost thirty years.

There had never been a need to.

He passed behind the head nurse's house and heard Eleanor in the kitchen. Cabinet doors were slammed repeatedly, and Ken shook his head. The ghost never grew tired of it, but Ken had.

As he neared the crematorium, the creak of a hinge told him someone else played with the iron door. The great oven hissed and crackled into life, even though the electricians had disconnected all of the power to it at the end of April.

They're on a roll tonight, he thought with a sigh. He exhaled and relaxed as best he could.

It was a little after one in the morning, and he still had almost six hours left in his shift.

"*Kenneth,*" a voice hissed.

Ken stopped and turned towards the voice.

The little girl with the stuffed dog stood behind the wrought iron fence.

"Hello," he said.

She narrowed her eyes and rage devoured her face. "*Watchman.*"

"Why?" Ken asked. "Why do you hate me so?"

For a brief moment, her eyes widened. "You don't remember me."

"I don't know you," Ken responded.

"You did," she said angrily. "You knew me well."

"When?"

"When you were younger," she said. "Much younger."

"How young?"

"I think you were five," she whispered. "Five. Five. Five. Not quite six."

Ken shook his head.

He could not remember her.

"And in your mother's garden, *Kenneth*, I heard the King," she said, whispering still. "I came and saw you, instead, playing amongst the flowers and beneath the apple tree. I spoke with you. I spoke with your mother. And my family burned, Watchman. They burned."

Ken remembered.

The Bordens.

The Bordens. The oldest daughter had watched him sometimes. She would sit with him while his mother worked around the house.

Her father had murdered her mother. Drowned her siblings. Set fire to the house and hung himself in the barn.

And Francine Borden had gone mad. Sent away.

To Middlebury.

"Francine," he whispered. "Francine. What happened?"

"The King happened!" she screamed, and the rage in her voice caused him to stagger back. "Sweet whispers in a nurse's ear and I too slipped free, Kenneth. Down and down and down into the tunnels, Kenneth. Down into the tunnels with my dog. My dog. My *Kenneth*. Named after my *favorite* little boy. The King is jealous, Kenneth. He will share you with no one. Not even a little girl."

"And I will see you dead before He has you, *Kenneth*," she said, her voice suddenly sweet. "I will see you dead."

She lifted the dog to her chest and stroked its head. Her lips were bloody as she smiled, her teeth coated as well. "Will you not join me here, Kenneth? Come, sit beside my grave and reminisce. We shall speak of your mother's garden, and of fire. Cold bath water and a hemp rope. Shall we?"

Ken cleared his throat uncomfortably. "I think not, Francine. But will you join me, in my house?"

A look of surprise crossed her face, and then she grinned devilishly at him. "No, Kenneth. No, Watchman. But I will see you. In the tunnels, where I died. We will see each other there."

Francine turned and walked away. She faded into the darkness, and Ken felt cold.

For a long time, he stood still, and he remembered the young girl who had played with him beneath the heavy boughs of the apple tree in his mother's garden.

CHAPTER 36
DENIED ACCESS

"Kenneth," the little girl said.

Oh, Jesus, Brian thought. *We don't need this.*

"Hello," Ken said.

"You aren't allowed up," she said, smirking. "You cannot come here. You have to keep walking."

"The door was open," Ken replied.

"But I have shut this one," she snapped.

Anne pressed herself closer to Brian.

"And the King?" Ken asked.

She spat on the floor. "Move further in, Kenneth. *Watchman.* I care not for the King nor for his Dog. I care not for Isabella, I care not. Move on and in, in and on. I will grant you death, should you climb these stairs."

"Fair enough," Ken said, turning around.

Brian followed suit and Anne asked, "Would she?"

"Of course, she would," Ken said. "She hates me."

Once again Ken took the lead in the tunnel. Their footsteps echoed oddly off of the walls and soon they were far from the girl and her dog.

"How much farther?" Brian asked.

"To the next building?" Ken said.

"Yeah," Brian said.

"In theory, ten minutes," Ken said.

"And in actuality, who knows?" Anne asked.

Ken chuckled uncomfortably. "Yes, young lady. I'm afraid you're absolutely correct."

"And the next door will be unlocked?" she asked.

"To a building? Yes."

"Will we find any open doors?" Brian asked.

"I would like to say 'no'," Ken said. "The truth, however, is we may well come across one."

"Do we avoid it?" Anne asked.

"No," Ken answered.

"No?" Anne said. "What do we do then?"

"We go in," Ken said in a resigned voice.

"Why?" Brian asked.

"Because it will mean Middlebury wants us to go in. And if we don't," Ken said, shrugging. "Well, let's say I've seen the same door five times in a row waiting for me and the others to enter. We would never reach another exit to the surface if we ignored an open door."

"Oh," Anne said. "What an absolutely horrible idea."

"Yes," Ken said.

The conversation stopped, and the three of them continued to walk. Their steps continued to echo, the beams of their flashlights continued to illuminate the seemingly endless tunnel. The path ran straight, curving neither to the left nor to the right. It grew warmer the further in they traveled and soon Brian had unzipped his coat and taken off his hat and gloves. He slipped the book into his shirt and tucked the hem back into his pants to keep the volume secure.

"Do you hear something?" Anne asked.

The three of them stopped, and Brian closed his eyes and listened intently.

"Yes," he said after a moment. "Yes. It sounds like a rocking chair."

"Exactly," Anne said, her tone excited. Brian couldn't tell if she was fearful or genuinely enthusiastic about the noise.

"Well," Ken said with a sigh. "I suppose we're going to find out."

He started down the tunnel and in a matter of moments his flashlight's beam fell upon an open door. Above the lintel, the number '1918' was printed in brilliant silver.

Ken paused at the threshold, and then he walked in, and Brian followed with Anne close behind.

The room took Brian by surprise.

He wasn't sure what he had been expecting, but the long, well-decorated apartment certainly hadn't been anywhere on the list of possibilities.

The scene before him looked as though it had come out of the early twentieth century. Tall, elegantly carved bookcases were placed symmetrically around the room with a large, wide fireplace occupying the center of the far wall. A fire burned pleasantly and cast out the perfect amount of heat. A few club chairs upholstered in dark brown leather framed small tables and elegant floor lamps with exquisite shades of stained glass gave off a soft light. In a shadow to the right of the fireplace, a hidden figure sat in a rocking chair and slowly rocked.

From what Brian could see, the person in the chair wore a pair of neatly pressed slacks and highly polished brown shoes. A tall table to the left supported a rather large decanter of alcohol and was accompanied by a tumbler half-filled with the same.

"Well," a rough, hoarse voice said from the rocker, "the Watchman has arrived."

"I have," Ken said in a low voice.

"And it is well you have." The person in the chair continued to rock gently. A gloved hand slipped out of the shadow, took hold of the tumbler and brought it back into darkness. A sound reminiscent of a dog drinking drowned out the rocker and the fire for a moment and then the tumbler was returned to the table.

"My apologies," the stranger said. "I know my habits will be disturbing to you. Please, sit, Watchman, and your guests as well. I believe Mr. Roy has a book?"

His name spoken in the strange place released curls of fear through Brian and caused him to shake slightly.

The stranger chuckled. "You've no fear from me, Brian Roy. All eyes are upon the Watchman, now. Even your pretty friend is safe from the ravagers abroad. We await the King, and the Watchman, of course."

Anne's hand found Brian's and he held onto it.

"Bring out your book, Mr. Roy," the stranger said. "For while time is fluid, it is not infinite, even in this place."

Brian continued to hold Anne's delicate hand as he put his flashlight down and he freed the book from his shirt.

"Sit, please, all of you," the stranger said. Once more the gloved hand appeared, took the drink, and brought it into the shadows. The disturbing noise of the stranger drinking filled the room.

Brian, Ken, and Anne all sat down. Brian looked down at the book in his hands and read the title for the first time.

Interventions in the Ghosts of Middlebury Sanitarium. No author was listed.

"You'll want page sixty-eight, Mr. Roy," the stranger said.

Brian opened the book to page sixty-eight.

"Please," the stranger said, "read aloud."

Brian cleared his throat, looked at the chapter title, and started to read.

"'*Nineteen forty-five and the War's End:*

Not surprisingly Middlebury saw nearly a score of cases concerning battle-fatigued soldiers, sailors, and marines. Unfortunately, as we saw an influx of these, the supernatural aspect of Middlebury increased. A few of the dead were contacted, and our medium was informed of the arrival of one 'Septimus Rex,' the Sanitarium's undead king.

He proved to be an exceptionally powerful and difficult ghost to handle. He was responsible, we believe, for several suicides of previously stable residents. Also, we believe he was responsible for the accidental death of at least one security guard and the vanishing of several other residents. During this time, there were also reports of a large, black German Shepherd, although no physical evidence was discovered.

With the increase in resident fatalities and the injuring of numerous staff members, it was decided by the head doctor, Doctor Gregory Magnus, to seek the assistance of a professional in regards to the supernatural. Dr. Magnus was able to locate a young woman in Nashua. She willingly came up to the Sanitarium and Dr. Magnus confided in her his concerns regarding the King.

The young woman took on the job and requested she be locked in the House. Dr. Magnus warned her of the dangers of the House, of the ghost known as Isabella, and the young woman assured us she would be fine.

She emerged from the House three days later. She was exhausted and sick, but she assured us she was successful in banishing the King. She informed us the banishment would not last long, and he would eventually return at his full strength once more. She told us to inform her immediately, and she would assist the Sanitarium again.

She accepted no payment for the job done, and so Florence MacReady will forever be honored at Middlebury Sanitarium"

"Enough," the stranger said.

Brian stopped and swallowed dryly.

"Have you heard enough?" the stranger asked.

"What do you mean?" Anne asked. "A young woman in forty-five would have to be dead by now."

"Oh, she is," the stranger said with a chuckle. "She most certainly is. But since when has death stopped Florence, eh, Mr. Roy?"

Brian dropped the book to the floor.

"Brian?" Anne asked as Ken looked at him.

"Yes," the stranger said, sighing happily. "You understand, don't you, Brian?"

"Yes," Brian managed to say.

"Good," the stranger said. The rocking chair stopped, and the stranger stood up. He stepped out into the light.

"Oh Jesus," Brian whispered.

"No," the stranger said, "I am not the Christ, Mr. Roy, but I do feel as though I have suffered for the sins of man."

The stranger had once been a man, although whether he had been attractive or not Brian would never know. No one would.

The man's face was ruined.

Each cheek had a matching hole, and through them, Brian could see the teeth were gone, the tongue twisted. The man's eyes were absent, the eyelids sunken and permanently sealed. Only a pair of holes remained of the nose, the flesh raw and hideous. The hair had been burned from his head, and scars rippled across the top of the skull.

"Behold," the stranger said, his hoarse voice low, "the horrors of war. I am *un homme sans visage*, and beneath the hands of a loving nurse I was smothered. She could not bear to see me suffer, although I had no wish to die. She sought to free me, and yet bound me here forever.

"None of us leave this place," the stranger said with a mangled laugh. "None of us. And should the King succeed in His ascension, well, you will be welcome here at any time."

The stranger stepped back into the shadow and returned to the rocker.

"Now," the man said, "hasten unto Florence. Middlebury has yet to decide its own fate, whether to be ruled by the King or to cast its lot with Florence."

The chair started to rock.

"Leave," the man said with a sigh. "The sight of you sickens me, as I'm sure you are sickened by my own visage."

Ken stood first, and Brian and Anne did so quickly. They made their way to the door and paused as the man spoke again.

"And remember," the man said, "the King longs to see you, Watchman."

Ken's face was pale as he led them back into the tunnel. The door closed heavily behind them.

"Do you know where this Florence is?" Ken asked after a few moments of silence.

Brian nodded. "It may be tough getting her here. And I'm not particularly pleased with the idea of it."

"Doesn't matter," Ken said. "If she can stop the King, then we need her."

"Is he really bad?" Anne asked.

"He's worse than all of Middlebury combined," Ken said. "It's why he's the King."

CHAPTER 37

KEN, MAY 6TH, 1986

Ken had known for nearly twenty years about Middlebury's various ghosts and horrors. He knew them all, or so he had foolishly assumed.

With the passage of time came the reorganization and restructure of Middlebury Sanitarium. Advances were made in treatment programs, and while the beds were always full in the various units, they were now filled with people who truly needed assistance rather than ones merely shunted off by their families.

Some of those residents, men, and women whose families had abandoned them because of depression or anxiety, still remained. They were unable to live outside of the structured and regimented life of the Sanitarium.

Ken understood. He had grown accustomed to living on the campus. He liked his little house and the quietness it afforded him. He didn't have any neighbors to interrupt his daytime sleeping. He didn't have any neighbors at all, thankfully.

I can't concentrate tonight, he realized. He put a bookmark into his copy of Shakespeare's *The Tragedy of Coriolanus* and stretched out his legs. There was a slight chill in the air, and he had been forced to keep the door shut to the guardhouse for most of his shift. It was five, though, and the sun kissed the horizon. Soon the great orb would rise and shine upon the earth and Middlebury alike, and Ken would go to bed shortly thereafter.

The phone rang, and Ken nearly jumped out of his chair.

He answered it.

"Security."

"Ken, this is Sue Jeffries in Four."

"Hi Sue," Ken said, straightening up. "What's going on?"

"I've got a resident out of bed and possibly out of the building," she said, her tone one of anxiousness.

"When?" Ken said, standing.

"Maybe five minutes ago," she answered. "I did a surprise sweep back through, and it looks like he slipped away between the first check and the second."

"Okay, not too bad," Ken said soothingly. "Who is it?"

"Mickey Verranault," Sue said.

Ken closed his eyes for a moment and placed the name with a face.

"About seventy? Bipolar manic depression?" Ken asked.

"Yeah," Sue said. "From what I remember he usually heads out just after lights out and not so late in the morning, when he gets out he likes to go to the boneyard."

"Got it. Thanks, Sue. I'll have my radio, and I'll call you shortly."

"Thanks, Ken," she said. "I'm sorry, we're short staffed tonight."

"Don't worry about it," Ken said. "Bye now."

He hung up the phone, turned to leave and yelled as he stumbled back.

Mickey Verranault was standing at the door and looking in.

"Jesus, Mickey," Ken said, opening the door. "You scared the hell out of me."

"Can I come in, Ken?" Mickey asked. His voice trembled, and his eyes darted around crazily.

"Sure, come on in," Ken said, gesturing to his chair.

Mickey shuffled in. He wore his slippers and his pajamas as well as a thick blue robe tied tightly around his narrow waist. Mickey's gray hair was long, well past his shoulders and his stubble only accentuated the sharp features of his face. As Mickey sat down and Ken closed the door, the older man hid his bony hands in the sleeves of his bathrobe.

"Just let me call over to Sue, okay?" Ken asked, reaching for the phone.

"Don't. Please, Ken," Mickey said. "Give me a few minutes."

The desperation in the man's voice stopped Ken's hand. Cautiously Ken leaned back against the wall and folded his arms across his chest. "What's going on?"

Mickey chewed on his lip nervously for a moment and then he finally said, "You know He's coming?"

"Who?" Ken asked.

"Septimus Rex," Mickey replied.

"How do you know about the King?" Ken asked in a soft voice.

"I just learned," Mickey said, tears welling up in his eyes. "Oh, Ken, I just learned. They told me. Yes, they told me. They said soon the King would come when the weather was cold, and when the Watchman was alone, the King would come."

"Is there anything else they told you?" Ken asked. He felt uncomfortable, as though he was being watched.

Mickey nodded as he started to hiccup and cry.

"What, Mickey?"

"They said don't bring her back," the old man whispered.

"Don't bring who back?" Ken asked.

Mickey shook his head. "They didn't say her name. Just not to bring her."

"Okay," Ken said. "Okay. Thank you for telling me."

"You're welcome," Mickey said, and he cried harder.

"Mickey," Ken said gently. "Mickey, why are you crying?"

"I can't leave!" Mickey moaned, looking up at Ken in terror. "Oh, Ken, I can't leave!"

The phone rang, and Mickey continued to sob. Ken reached over the man and answered the phone.

"Security," Ken said.

"Oh Ken," Sue said, her voice thick, "I'm glad I caught you. Marianne from the first floor, she went out to check the boneyard, and she found Mickey. He's dead, Ken. He fell and hit his head on a marker, and he's dead."

"Okay, Sue," Ken said numbly. "I'll be right there."

He hung up the phone, stepped back and looked at Mickey.

Mickey continued to cry.

"You're dead?" Ken said.

Mickey nodded.

"And now you can't leave."

"I can't leave!" Mickey said, becoming frantic. "I can't leave, Ken. I can't leave. *I can't leave!*"

The window in the door shattered and a blast of cold air raced through Ken.

"It's okay," Ken said, gathering his thoughts. "You can always come and see me. Do you understand?"

Mickey nodded, wiped his nose with the cuff of his robe and said, "Are you sure?"

Ken smiled. "I'm sure. I have to go to the boneyard right now. You can stay here if you want."

"I will," Mickey said, a small smile appearing on his face. "You bet I will."

"Good," Ken said. "I'm glad. I'll be back soon, Mickey."

"Okay, Ken," Mickey said happily, and he started to rock in the chair.

With a sigh, Ken opened the door, stepped over the broken glass and made his way to the boneyard to gather up Mickey's body.

CHAPTER 38
MAKING A CALL

Brian sat in the kitchen of Ken's house.

His cell phone wouldn't send texts or make calls. He couldn't use it to piggy-back a signal so he could email from his laptop.

Luckily he could still access his contacts. Even luckier still, Ken had a landline.

And it was working.

Not only was the phone hard-lined into the system, but the phone itself was a rotary. An old, mustard yellow wall job with a cord an easy thirteen feet in length.

Whatever, so long as it works, Brian thought with a sigh. He brought Charles Gottesman's number up and dialed it. The click of the rotary reminded him of his childhood, the memories cut off as the phone started to ring on the other end.

The phone rang three times before Ellen picked up and said, "Hello?"

"Ellen, it's Brian Roy."

"Oh," she laughed. "I had no idea who it could be. The caller ID was saying it was the Middlebury Sanitarium."

"Well, I'm at Middlebury," Brian said, trying to keep his voice light.

"Seriously?" she asked. "I thought they had closed the place down."

"They did. I'm on a job. And, actually, I called to ask a favor of you and Charles."

"Sure," she said. "What's up?"

"I was wondering if one of you could bring Florence up here," Brian said, wincing as he asked.

Ellen paused for a long time before responding.

"You want Florence?"

"Yes," Brian said.

"Why?" Ellen's tone was sharp and cold.

"There's something bad going on here," Brian said. "Something terrible. There's a thing coming. Septimus Rex. The King. We also found a book here, and it says the only person who ever successfully banished this King before was Florence."

"And you think she'll do it again?" Ellen asked skeptically.

"All I can do is hope," Brian said. "But the information we've received is 'yes,' she'll do it."

"You're risking a lot," Ellen said. "A real lot. She gets loose, and there'll be hell to pay."

"I know," Brian said with a sigh, "and I don't like it."

"Well," Ellen said, "let me talk with Charles. If he thinks you're out of your mind, we'll call back. If not, we'll be there soon."

"Listen," Brian said, "I'll ask the security guard to meet you at the gate. Do not come in here, Ellen. No matter what. Okay?"

Ellen paused and then she asked, "Is it really bad?"

"It's terrible," Brian answered. "Absolutely terrible."

"Alright then," she said. "Good luck."

"Thanks," Brian said, and he hung up the phone.

Now he had to talk with Ken and hope Charles would bring Florence up.

CHAPTER 39
ALONE IN THE HOUSE

When Brian had talked to Ken about going out and meeting the Gottesmans, Ken had readily agreed. This left Anne alone in the house with Brian. Under different circumstances she might have gone over and spoken to him about the way she felt.

As it was, she was barely able to control herself.

The entire adrenaline rush of the situation had kicked her hormones into overdrive, and she had to force herself to remain in her seat.

There was entirely too much space open on the couch.

Entirely too much couch to begin with.

The butterflies in her stomach were a mixture of fear and raw sexuality, and if Brian even walked by her, she wasn't sure if she would be able to contain herself.

And it looked as though Brian felt the same. He stole glances at her out of the corner of his eye and seemed to have been reading the same page from Dashiell Hammett mystery for the past ten minutes.

Anne closed her eyes and tried to focus on the situation outside of the house rather than the one in it.

The King is coming, Anne told herself. *Someone named Florence is dead, and she's coming. I'm surrounded by the dead. By things, I really wasn't quite sure of when I pulled into the Sanitarium this morning.*

The sound of movement caused her to open her eyes. Brian stood up, went to a window, looked out of it and sighed. He turned away from it, smiled at Anne and walked towards her. He dropped his hand down as he passed and lightly caressed her arm.

The thrill it sent through her caused goose bumps to ripple across her skin.

Oh, Brian, don't touch me, she thought desperately.

Brian walked to a back window and looked out of it. He shook his head a moment later and rubbed his chin.

"Something wrong?" Anne asked. "I mean, other than the obvious stuff?"

He glanced over his shoulder and smiled at her, and Anne understood how Jenny could have fallen in love with the man. There was something perfect about his smile. Unguarded and inoffensive.

"It's the dead," he said, returning to his seat. He looked tired and worn out.

"What about them?" Anne asked.

"They're here."

"I know," she said.

He chuckled. "No. I mean they're here, at the house."

"What?" she asked, sitting up a little straighter.

"Outside of the house," Brian said. "They've formed a ring. They must be at least ten or fifteen deep. Maybe more."

"What about Ken?" Anne asked. "Will he be okay?"

"Yes," Brian said. "I don't think anyone except the King would interfere with Ken at this point. Some of them may not like him. Some of them may actually wish to harm him. But with the King's arrival imminent, I think they're too afraid. Ken should be able to meet with Florence without any of the dead giving him a hard time."

"Who is Florence?" Anne said. "I meant to ask you earlier."

"Florence," Brian said, taking a deep breath and letting it out slowly. "Florence is a nightmare."

And Anne listened as Brian began to speak about Florence, Leo, Paul, and the Kenyon Farm.

CHAPTER 40

KEN AND AN OLD FRIEND

Ken heard him before he saw him.

Someone kept pace with him, a short distance behind.

A look over his shoulder had shown nothing, but it was Middlebury. There could have been a marching band ready to play, and Ken wouldn't see them if they didn't want him to.

Of course, a marching band of the dead was a ridiculous image, and he let out a snort of laughter.

He paused and dug out his pipe and tobacco. The old routine calmed him as he packed the bowl, the interior of the briarwood dark with years of use.

I'll have to clean this soon, Ken thought. *If I get the chance to ever clean anything again.*

The rustle of clothes caught his ears, and Ken looked up as he put the tobacco away and found his lighter.

Mickey Verranault stood on the road a few feet ahead of him.

Mickey looked the same as he had all those years before when he had visited Ken at the guardhouse.

"Hello, Mickey," Ken said conversationally, lighting his pipe. He took several deep breaths, made sure the tobacco was fully lit and dropped the lighter back into his pocket.

"Hi, Ken," Mickey said. He squinted. "You're old."

Ken chuckled. "You're no spring chicken yourself, Mickey."

"But I won't get any older," Mickey said sadly.

"I might not either," Ken said soberly, realizing, for the first time the end truly could be near for him. Who knew what the plan of the King entailed.

"I don't know about how old you'll get," Mickey said. He scratched at the back of his head.

"So," Ken said, exhaling a cloud of smoke. "To what do I owe this pleasant surprise?"

"I came to tell you to be careful," Mickey said in a low voice. "You know the King is coming."

It wasn't a question.

Ken nodded.

"And you're getting ready to get help," Mickey continued.

"How do you know about it?" Ken asked.

"Clyde told me," Mickey whispered.

"Who's Clyde?" Ken said.

"Clyde lives in the tunnels," Mickey said confidentially. "You met him. His face is gone, poor Clyde. It wasn't even the Germans. An artillery round from the French fell short. Poor Clyde. I like Clyde. He's always nice to me. He even lets me hide in his room sometimes, when the bad ones are out."

"The bad ones?" Ken asked.

Mickey nodded. "You know the bad ones. The ones Isabella likes. Ones like Francine. Bad, bad, *bad ones*."

"Yes," Ken said, thinking about both the girl and the woman. "The bad ones."

"Some of the bad ones," Mickey said, "they don't want you to bring help. They await the coming of the King. Be careful, Ken. Be very careful."

"I will," Ken said seriously. "Thank you, Mickey."

"You're welcome," Mickey said, glancing around nervously. "You were always nice to me. Always. I'm going to go back to Clyde's. It's quiet there. And safe."

And Mickey vanished, and Ken choked on his smoke at the suddenness of it.

Ken cleared his throat and started again on the road towards the guardhouse. He didn't know when the people would show up with Florence, but he needed to be ready.

CHAPTER 41

KEN, SEPTEMBER 2ND, 1998

Ken found the Honda Civic parked behind Building One.

The engine was still warm, and the car was empty. A quick look inside showed three McDonald's cups with condensation on them.

Three, Ken thought. He turned his flashlight away from the car. *Three.*

They could be anywhere. The cemetery. One of the buildings. One of the residences.

God help them if they're in the tunnels, Ken thought.

He walked around Building One and checked the windows of the basement and the first floor. He made sure the doors were secure, and then he moved on to Building Two where he repeated the process. Buildings Three and Four were fine. The library and the chow hall. The maintenance building and the crematorium as well. His own house was untouched, Isabella's and the Head Nurse's and the Superintendent's homes all stood pristine.

Only the sheds remained.

The stairs into the tunnels.

He found the doors closed and locked.

Middlebury didn't want the strangers in its tunnels.

A horrified scream tore through the air.

The boneyard, Ken thought as he turned. He started to jog towards the cemetery. Another scream broke free only to suddenly be cut off.

Ken sighed tiredly.

Too late.

He slowed back down to a walk.

No more screams issued forth from the boneyard. They would either be dead, or close to it. Middlebury had not been forgiving of late.

Ken had found a transient dead in the maintenance building at the beginning of August. Halfway through July, he had picked up over a hundred dead Canadian geese. Each neck had been twisted, so the bird had looked along its own back. The wings had all been broken.

No, something at the Sanitarium was angry. Angrier than usual.

Francine stood near the cemetery's gates. She held her stuffed dog in one hand, the other hand behind her back. She glared at Ken.

Ken stopped and looked at her. "Hello."

"*Kenneth*," she said, her voice heavy with anger.

"I heard some screams," he said. "I came to find out why."

"You would have heard more," she said, her voice suddenly sweet. "But we didn't want to disturb you."

"How did you stop the screaming?" Ken asked, afraid of the answer.

Francine smiled happily as she brought the hidden hand out before her. She held some bloody meat out to him.

"What are those?" he asked politely, quelling the roiling bile in his stomach.

"Tongues," she said happily. "They can moan and groan, but they cannot scream, Watchman. Not without their tongues."

"How many?"

"Just two," she said with a smile.

"What about the third?" he asked.

Her eyes widened. "How did you know?"

Ken shrugged.

"We killed him," she snapped. "He had a pistol. He made us angry. And besides, Ike said it would be better."

Ken stiffened at the name of his old friend and partner.

"Ike?" Ken asked.

She nodded. "He doesn't want us to play with them. He doesn't want you to get in trouble. He told us to kill the one with the gun. Then we could kill the others with it once we had our fun."

"Where is he?" Ken said.

"Ike is dead," Francine replied.

"I know he's dead," Ken said, keeping tight control upon his temper. "Where is he?"

"Probably with Clyde," Francine said dismissively. She looked at the tongues in her hands. "I'll have to bring these to Isabella. She'll be very happy."

"Who's Clyde?" Ken asked.

"Too many questions, *Kenneth!*" she shrieked. "Too many! Clyde is Clyde and Ike is with him. I must bring Isabella her gift. The intruders are in the boneyard. One of who is gone and two more who shall join him soon!"

Francine turned away and stormed off towards Isabella's.

Ken looked at the boneyard's gate and felt sick as he heard a groan. With a deep breath, he walked forward and followed the slim path among the headstones and markers.

A moment later he was upon them.

They were young. Perhaps teens, maybe twenty-somethings. One was dead, propped up against a stone with a gun in his hand. He had an expression of pure horror on his face. He had been a handsome youth, tall and well built. His clothes were fashionable and splattered with blood.

Two young women lay on the ground, stripped down to their bare flesh.

Something had beaten them, and bruises had already started to form on them. One of the girls whimpered, and Ken stepped towards her.

"Hold, Watchman," a voice said.

Ken turned towards the corpse of the young man and saw a dark shape slip into the corpse. The arm with the pistol raised up, the thumb cocked the weapon and pointed it at Ken.

"They die," the voice said, still beside the man.

"No," Ken said, taking another step towards the young women.

"They die," the voice repeated, and the corpse fired the gun.

Ken staggered back as something punched him in the left shoulder. He felt blood soak his shirt as he collapsed to his knees.

The gun barked twice more, and Ken didn't need to see the mutilated women to know they had been killed.

He felt numbness wrap over him, and Ken knew it was shock. The knowledge chased him into darkness.

CHAPTER 42
IN THE HOUSE

"And you're bringing her here?" Anne asked.

Brian looked at her, stuffed his attraction for her into the back of his thoughts and nodded. "Yes."

"Because she beat the King once before?"

"Yes."

"And because a faceless, literally faceless ghost said it, she was our best bet?" Anne said.

Brian sighed. "Yes."

Anne shook her head. "This is absolutely insane. And not the whole ghost part. I get the ghost part. But... but I... oh, I don't know. I really don't know."

"Try not to think about it," Brian said. "At least, not until it's over."

Anne breathed slowly and looked at him steadily. "She tried to kill you when you were in the hospital room."

"She did indeed," Brian said.

"What's to stop her from trying again?"

"Nothing," Brian said. "All I can hope is she's more intent on beating the King again than she is on punishing me."

"You're taking a hell of a chance," Anne said.

"You don't have to stay here, Anne," Brian said in a soft voice. "You can go home."

She looked at him steadily, and then she smiled broadly. Brian felt the attraction between the two of them leap across the room.

"No," she said, closing her eyes and resting her head against the back of her chair. "You know I can't."

And Brian remained silent because he knew she couldn't.

CHAPTER 43
AT THE GUARDHOUSE

At midnight, a car slowed down and turned into the entrance of Middlebury Sanitarium. The headlights cut a bright swath through the darkness as the vehicle came to a stop near the guardhouse.

Ken didn't put the book down. He didn't take his pipe out of his mouth.

He hadn't been able to read or smoke as he had waited.

He was worried.

For the first time in over four decades at the Sanitarium, Ken was worried.

The King was coming.

Ken stepped out of the guardhouse and as he did so, the driver's side door to the car opened.

"Close the door," Ken said firmly.

The door closed, and the window went down as Ken walked closer. The driver cut the headlights, and the passenger turned on the interior light.

Ken stopped at the open window and crouched down to smile at the two people. The driver was a man around Brian's age, the woman somewhat older than Anne. She held a small wooden box on her lap.

"Hello," the driver said. "I'm Charles, and this is my wife, Ellen."

"Ellen, Charles," Ken said. "A pleasure. My name's Ken. Brian asked me to wait here for you."

Charles looked out at Middlebury, the campus illuminated only by moonlight, which reflected brightly on the snow. After a moment, he returned his attention to Ken.

"This place is bad," Charles said. "You should deliver the box and get home."

"Thank you," Ken said, sincerely. "But Middlebury is my home. I've lived on-site since nineteen sixty-nine."

Ellen whistled appreciatively.

"You've managed to be here all this time?" Charles asked in surprise.

"Yes," Ken said.

"Bless you," Charles said. "I'm impressed."

"Thank you," Ken said.

Charles turned to Ellen, who nodded and handed him the box. Charles passed it through the window to Ken, who took it carefully.

"My suggestion," Charles said, "is not to open the box until you absolutely need to. Florence is extremely powerful. She always gives me a hell of a time at home."

"I'm not exactly sad to see her go," Ellen said, "but I don't want anything bad to happen up here either."

"So be careful," Charles continued. "She may help you, or she may be spiteful and refuse. Hell, she may well turn around and help whoever it is you want her to take care of."

"Yeah," Ken said with a sigh. "The last part wouldn't surprise me at all. Not here."

"Just be cautious. Please," Charles said.

"I will," Ken said. He straightened up and took a step away from the car. "Drive safely. It was a pleasure to meet you both."

"Likewise," Charles said.

Ellen reached up and turned off the interior light. Charles rolled up the window, turned on the lights and backed out of the driveway and onto the main road. Charles beeped the horn once, and Ken waved. He waited a moment for the rear lights to disappear into the night before he returned to the guardhouse.

Once inside, he put the box down on the desk and looked at it.

The wooden container was no larger than a shoebox, yet it had felt as though someone had filled it with lead weights. It didn't have a lock, although there was a pair of brass hinges.

Ken had no urge whatsoever to open the box.

He would prefer to not even be at Middlebury when it was opened, but he knew such an option was not on the table.

Well, he thought, picking the box back up, *best to get this thing to Brian. He'll know what to do with it now.*

Ken left the guardhouse and started along the road back towards his house.

The Sanitarium was unnaturally quiet.

Over the years, he had grown used to the natural silence. No longer did he filter out the screams and cries of residents. Rather he listened for sounds just under those of the wind and the night animals, the creak of buildings as they slowly settled into old age.

Yet Ken heard nothing.

Not a single owl. No foxes. No scurry of mice beneath the snow or hares upon it. The buildings themselves were mute. Each of his own steps, however, were painfully clear. His breath dissipated quickly, and the beat of his own heart was a drum upon which a madman hammered.

"Where goest thou, my love?" a voice said softly from behind him.

Ken stopped and turned around.

Isabella stood in the center of the road. Her hands were clasped politely in front of her, and she smiled affectionately at him.

"Hello, Isabella," Ken said with a short bow.

"Watchman," she said with a smile. "Where goest thou?"

"I'm returning home," Ken replied.

"And with what, pray tell?" she asked.

"A gift for my guests," he answered.

"Is it wise," she said, her voice taking on a chilling note, "for you to bring such a 'gift' into the domain of our King?"

Terror ran through Ken. The memories of the men in the cellar, the rats.

"I must, Isabella," Ken said. "So with your permission, dear lady, I must return."

"But you do not have it," she said, her tone harsh. "You do not have my permission, Kenneth. Not the smallest amount of it."

And Isabella launched herself at him.

Ken turned to run but stumbled. He fell, and the box flew from his hand to land heavily upon the asphalt.

The lid sprang open as Isabella surged past him towards the box and darkness poured out of it.

Isabella screamed as she was knocked backward.

Ken scrambled to his feet even as Isabella leaped up once more.

But the darkness enveloped the woman and she shrieked.

Ken watched, transfixed by what he saw.

Whatever had come out of the box seemed to form into a thousand hooks. Each sank into Isabella, her hair and her skin, her clothes and her teeth. Ken watched as they started to pull her apart. Flesh tore as easily as fabric, teeth popped with a sound similar to the eyes as they were pulled free.

Ken staggered back, collapsed to one knee and vomited the bit of toast and coffee he had managed to eat earlier.

Isabella's shrieks ended suddenly with an almost audible click.

With the back of his mitten, Ken wiped his mouth and looked up.

A tall, elegant, and powerful woman stood before him. She looked sternly at him for a moment, and then her gaze softened.

"Watchman," she said in a voice he had heard decades earlier, "is it time?"

Ken could only nod.

Mrs. Smith stood before him.

CHAPTER 44

KEN, AUGUST 27TH, 1973

The past week had been difficult.

Two residents had vanished into the woods. Well, the theory was they had vanished into the woods.

The reality was no one knew how they had even gotten out of their ward. They had been on the top floor of Building Three, each secure in a separate room. At the six pm check, they had been there.

At the seven pm check, they had been gone.

Windows secure. Doors secure. All of the alarms worked.

Two teams of the second shift had worked through the area between six and seven and in the bright, late evening light of August they hadn't seen anything.

No one, in fact, had seen anything.

The only change had been to the residents prior to them disappearing.

Both of the men were from the top floor of Building Three. Both of them had a history of violence, yet each had become quiet and fearful over the days previous to their vanishing, as though they waited for something.

They had disappeared on Monday.

Tuesday saw a slew of suicides.

One in each of the resident buildings.

Wednesday saw an entire ward in Building Two mutilate themselves. Each had carved a number into their chest. The resident in bed one carved the Roman numeral one, and the other residents had followed suit all the way up to the number forty-two.

Thursday witnessed a murder, which while not unheard of in Middlebury's past, was still relatively rare. A girl of ten had choked a cook to death during lunch.

And now it's Friday, Ken thought. He punched in and wondered numbly what the night would bring. He had worked overtime all week, long mornings spent in the woods on the trails. No evidence of the missing residents.

He walked back out in the warm August air and looked at the moths as they fluttered around the lamps.

"Ken!" a voice called.

Ken turned and saw Gus.

Gus moved towards him, and a tall, elegant woman of perhaps fifty walked beside him. She wore a lightweight dress of dark gray, her black hair was coiffed perfectly upon her head, and she gave Ken a brilliant smile.

Ken walked towards them and when they met she extended her hand. Ken shook it.

"Ken," Gus said, and the woman cut him off gently.

"Mrs. Smith," she said.

Gus shot her a confused look, but he didn't say anything contrary.

"Ken Buckingham," Ken said. "A pleasure, ma'am."

Her smile broadened.

"I work with other facilities," she said, glancing at Gus, "and Gus informed me of Middlebury's security concerns this morning."

"We've been working all day," Gus added. "But I believe Mrs. Smith has gotten a handle on the situation."

She nodded. "I have. And you needn't worry about finding the missing residents. Unfortunately, we found them this morning, down a ravine to the north."

"At least, they're found," Ken said. "Have we figured out how they managed to get out?"

"One of the other residents," Mrs. Smith said. "Somehow a key was pilfered, and the doors were opened. Gus will be instituting a stricter accounting of the keys during each shift."

Ken glanced at Gus, but his boss said nothing. Gus seemed, in fact, to be perfectly fine with whatever Mrs. Smith said.

"Well," Ken said, "sounds fantastic to me. The fewer residents who get out will be better."

"Too much work?" Mrs. Smith asked.

"No," Ken said with a smile. "I worry about them. They have it tough enough. Them getting out adds an element of risk I'd rather they not take."

"Well spoken," Mrs. Smith said. "Now I know you must be on your way, but it was a sincere pleasure."

She extended her hand again, and once more Ken shook it.

"Likewise, Mrs. Smith."

"Take care, Watchman," she said, and she and Gus walked to Building One.

Ken made his way to the guardhouse and at the door he stopped and straightened up.

Watchman, he thought. *She called me Watchman.*

He turned and stared at the building. Gus and Mrs. Smith had already gone into the building, however, and Ken knew he shouldn't follow.

His hand trembled as he opened the door of the guardhouse to get a flashlight and a radio.

He needed to start his shift.

CHAPTER 45
AN EXPLANATION... OF SORTS

Ken got to his feet and stared at Mrs. Smith.

"Mrs. Smith," he said, shaking his head.

She was older, perhaps another twenty years older than the first and only time he had seen her. But it was undeniably Mrs. Smith.

She smiled at him. A genuinely pleased smile.

"No, Kenneth," she said, her voice powerful. "My name is not Mrs. Smith, as I'm sure you knew when we first met. My name is Florence, and it will be enough if you call me so."

"Thank you, Florence," Ken said.

"You are not the one who sought my help, are you?" she asked. "For my jailers said it was a heathen named Brian."

"Brian is the one who asked for you, Florence," Ken said. "But he did so because of a book."

She frowned. "A book?"

Ken nodded.

"What book, Kenneth?" she asked.

Ken wracked his memory for a moment and then he said, "I think it was titled, Interventions in the Ghosts of Middlebury."

"Ah," she said, nodding. "So they did write it down. Excellent. I take it then, Kenneth, you are expecting the imminent arrival of the King?"

"Yes," he said, and the thought terrified him.

"Bring me to Brian then," she said, the man's name seeming to be distasteful to her. "I would speak with him."

"Alright," Ken said. "I think you'll have to wait outside of my house, though."

"Why?" she asked.

"Ghosts can't seem to get into my house."

"Don't worry, Kenneth," she said with a smile, "I'm the one who made it so. Your door will open for me."

Ken swallowed nervously and started to walk home.

Florence walked beside him, and they left the open box on the side of the road.

CHAPTER 46
BETTER TIMES HAVE BEEN FORGOTTEN

Anne had fallen asleep on the couch, and Brian sat in Ken's recliner. In Ken's cabinets he had found a bottle of bourbon. He considered liquor to be medicinal and poured himself a healthy dose.

For possibly the twentieth time Brian took out his cell phone and saw, again, he had no reception. He had even tried to call Jenny from Ken's landline, but for some reason, his calls went directly to voicemail. Either there was a problem with the carrier or her phone registered the Middlebury Sanitarium as an unknown caller and shunted the call away.

Regardless as to why it happened, Brian still couldn't get in touch with Jenny.

And temptation lay on the couch across from him.

The desperate nature of their venture, the undeniable attraction he and Anne felt towards one another, increased his desire to touch her.

Thankfully the bourbon cut into the passion in his breast and allowed him to get better control of himself.

Brian took another drink and then swirled the golden fluid around the bottom of the glass. The smell was heady, and he closed his eyes to enjoy it. After a moment, he finished the drink, put the empty glass on the coffee table and stood up. His legs wobbled slightly, and it took him a second to get his balance.

With a sigh, he crossed the room to the front door and peered out at the side lights.

The dead lined the road and stared at the house. They even lined the brick path. They stood impassively in the snow.

In the moonlight, a short way down the road, Brian saw two figures. They walked steadily, and as they neared the house, Brian recognized Ken.

And Florence.

Brian took an involuntary step back. His heart started its irregular beat and for the first time at Middlebury, he wondered if he had remembered to pack his heart medication.

It won't matter, he told himself. *Not if she doesn't want it to matter.*

Brian made his way back to the chair and sat down so heavily it woke Anne up.

She sat up bleary eyed and looked around slightly confused.

"Brian?" she asked, stifling a yawn. She looked at him and sleep fled her eyes. "Brian, are you okay?"

He shook his head and pointed to the front door.

Anne frowned, stood up and went to the door. Like him, Anne peered out the side lights.

"I see Ken and a woman," Anne said, looking back to Brian. "Is she the one with Florence?"

"No," Brian whispered.

"No?" Anne asked

"No."

"Who is it then?" she said, turning around to look at him.

"Florence," Brian said. "She's Florence."

"What?" Anne said, glancing out again. "What? Why is she out? I thought she was supposed to be contained until it was time to face the King?"

"I don't know," Brian said. "I don't know why she's out."

Anne hurried back to the couch and sat down. "She can't come in, right? Didn't you say this was a safe place? Ghosts can't come in?"

Relief flooded through Brian, and he sagged back into the chair. "You're right. I had forgotten. Oh thank God, I'd forgotten."

Anne smiled.

A key turned in the lock and then the front door swung open. Ken smiled at them as cold air rushed into the warm house and he stepped aside, and Florence crossed the threshold.

"Hello Brian," she said, her voice harsh. "I'm quite surprised you asked to see me."

Brian's heart skipped a beat and the world went black.

CHAPTER 47
WHEN WILL THE KING ARRIVE?

The air ripped open, and Septimus Rex stepped out of the shadows and into Isabella's parlor.

His young mistress was not home.

The fire in her hearth was dead.

The tortured in her basement were silent.

Rage flitted through his thoughts. Someone had robbed him of his woman, his company, the sole soul who understood and obeyed.

The house felt his anger and the horsehair plaster burst into flame around him. The wooden floor and the rag-rugs scorched and then they burned as he walked upon them. With a gesture from his hand the front door exploded outward. Splinters shot out into the night.

When the King exited the house, even the bricks began to burn. In the yard, the snow melted at his presence. The old apple tree withered and died as it sank in upon itself.

Middlebury's imprisoned dead, his unwilling subjects, cowered along the brick path and filled the street. He smiled at them, a smile which sent many of the dead into terrified sobs.

Many, but not all.

A young girl stood at the intersection of the walkway and the asphalt. In one hand she held a stuffed toy. The girl glared at him with hate.

It pleased him, and Septimus Rex smiled benignly at her.

"My dear," he said, stopping a short distance from her, "will you not pay homage to your liege?"

The girl curtsied and spat vehemently upon the ground.

"Do you know," he asked, "how my mistress died?"

"I do," the girl answered, straightening up.

Her hate was pure, and Septimus Rex admired her for it.

"Will you tell me?" he asked, chuckling.

"Of course," the girl said. She smiled at him. "She died by the hands of your watchman."

Mirth fled from the King.

"I have no time for jokes, young lady," he said sternly. "I do not enjoy them."

"It was no joke, Septimus Rex," she replied, "and, in all honesty, I do not care what you enjoy."

Septimus' rage boiled up, and he pushed it back. "Tell me then, and quickly."

The girl paused for a long moment and just as the King was about to speak again she said, "It was the stranger and the watchman."

"What stranger?" Septimus Rex demanded.

"A strange man sent to study Middlebury," the girl answered. "The watchman went to fetch a box from him and in the box, there was a killer. When the box was opened, well, Isabella died."

"And my watchman did this?" Septimus Rex asked, with fury building within him.

"Yes," the girl said happily.

"How did my mistress die?" he asked.

"Miserably," the girl said. "More's the pity. I did like her. I had wished the watchman had killed you rather than Isabella."

Septimus Rex snarled, and his anger escaped him. It rolled out in a wave along the path. The dead shrieked as it passed them, for although the rage was directed at the girl the mere closeness of the rage burned them.

And when his fury struck her, the girl laughed.

She laughed even as she was ripped apart. Flesh from muscle, muscle from bone, organs desiccated. Although she was dead, she felt every bit of pain as though she was alive.

A moment later only the stuffed dog and her tattered night shirt remained.

Septimus Rex looked at the other dead around him. No one met his eyes. No head was raised.

"I go now to my watchman," the King said. "To hear if her accusations were true."

The bricks cracked beneath his feet as he walked along the path. He paused at the remnants of the girl's nightshirt and picked up the dog.

Yes, the King thought, looking at the dog. *I will ask my watchman if what this one had said was true.*

With the toy tucked under his arm the King started towards the watchman's home.

CHAPTER 48

WITH THE WATCHMAN

Fear kept Brian in the recliner.

He had only been unconscious for a few minutes, enough time to scare Anne. Ken, however, was fully trained in CPR, and he had assured both Anne and Brian. Brian had only fainted. He had not suffered another heart attack.

Being ashamed of fainting is better than being dead, Brian told himself.

Ken sat on the couch beside Anne, and all three of them looked to the front door.

Florence stood there, and a small smile played upon her lips. Anne had read to her from the book that the ghost in the library had thrown at Brian.

Ken had told her about Clyde in the tunnel, of how they needed to call upon Florence.

Florence had listened to all of it quietly, and she seemed to absorb all of the information. When Ken finished, a silence had fallen over the house.

Brian had glanced at the front window once and seen the dead. They pressed close to see them and to see what Florence would do.

Brian was curious about her next decision as well.

He figured his chances of leaving the house alive were pretty slim.

"You know, Brian Roy," Florence said, her voice carrying with it a note of grim determination, "there are things in this world and the next that are far greater than either of us. Far more important than either of us can truly understand."

Suddenly Florence looked to the left, her eyes took on a faraway look, and a small, pleased smile crept over her face.

"Ah," she said, turning to look at them again. "The King approaches."

A burst of fear punched Brian in the stomach, and he nearly doubled over from the pain of it. He saw Anne's face go white and her throat convulsed. Ken stood up and walked around the room anxiously. Finally, the man turned and looked at Florence.

"Florence," Ken said respectfully, "will you be able to handle the King?"

"Alone?" she asked. "Possibly. With you, undoubtedly."

Ken looked confused. "With me?"

"Yes," Florence said, looking at him piercingly. "With you. You are the Watchman, Kenneth. And I ask you this, who were you watching over all these years?"

"The residents and staff of Middlebury, when there were residents," he said.

Florence smiled at him. "Kenneth, there are residents still. You know it to be true, and thus, you remained to continue to watch over them. Now I ask you this, were you watching over the residents for the benefit of the King?"

Ken shook his head.

"And why do you not serve the King?" Florence asked gently.

"Because the King keeps them here," Ken said. "He keeps them all here."

"Exactly," Florence said, nodding her head with approval. "Exactly. Together the King is ours, Ken. The fight will not be easy. But he will be ours. Do you believe me?"

"I do," Ken whispered. "I do."

"Come then, Kenneth, Brian, and Anne," Florence said. "Let us prepare to meet the King."

CHAPTER 49
EMBRACING DESTINY

Ken had been afraid before.

He had made it through Vietnam, after all. He had an airstrike medal with four clusters. Ken had even survived a helicopter crash and landed in zones so hot he thought he wouldn't see home again.

So yes, Ken knew fear.

But he hadn't known fear like this.

Beyond his own front door, the king approached.

Septimus Rex. An untouchable murderer.

Septimus Rex, who came to claim Ken as his own.

"Should I get my shotgun?" Ken asked Florence.

The dead woman looked at him, smiled and shook her head. "No, Kenneth. Such a thing will not work on the King."

"What will?" Brian asked.

The look Florence gave made Brian nervous.

She hated the man.

Brian looked down at his own feet.

Florence turned back to Ken.

"You'll know what to do, Watchman. Have no fear," she said. "Come now, all of you. It won't be safe in here."

"Can they get in?" Anne asked, clearly reluctant to leave the house.

"No," Florence said. "But they can destroy it."

"Oh," Anne said, standing up. "Okay then."

Ken watched Brian stand up as well. Ken turned to Florence and said, "I'm ready."

"Good," she said, and she opened the door.

At the end of his walkway, Ken saw the King.

Septimus Rex was a monster. Perhaps seven feet in height and proportionately built, the King wore a massive gray robe which looked to be the tattered remains of a hospital gown. His feet were wrapped in burlap sacks, and his hair was white and tufts of it clung to a nearly bald head. His face was fat, his eyes a bright blue. The teeth in his head were yellow with wide gaps between them.

And in a massive hand, he carried Francine's dog.

The stench of death permeated the cold air, and the King licked his lips with a vividly red tongue.

Florence stepped to one side, and Ken did the same. Anne and Brian followed close behind.

"Who summoned the woman?" the King asked, and his voice was deep, painful to Ken's ears.

"I did," Brian answered.

"I hate you," Septimus Rex said, and Brian screamed.

Ken turned to look at the other man, and he saw Brian was on fire. His clothes burned brightly as Anne slapped at the flames.

"Enough!" Ken yelled, and the flames went out.

The King looked surprised.

"Stronger than you thought, Septimus?" Florence asked.

The King stared angrily at her. "Keep your mouth closed, woman."

Florence laughed. "And what will you do, Septimus?"

"Septimus Rex!" the King screamed. "Do not forget my title!"

"Earn it," she said.

"I have earned it!"

Ken's house exploded, and the force of the blast threw him forward. Over the sound of the flames and of things popping in the sudden heat, Ken heard someone yell. He pulled himself up and looked around. Brian was on his knees, head down. From the man's shoulder, a large piece of wood, perhaps a foot long and an inch in diameter, protruded. Blood ran down Anne's face as she tried to help Brian to his feet.

Florence alone remained on her feet.

"Pretty," Florence said, and she made a small gesture with her hand.

The night, illuminated by the flames as they devoured Ken's home, rippled.

Septimus Rex stumbled back, shock clear on his face.

And for the first time Ken saw a flicker of fear cross the King's face.

"Did you think, Septimus," Florence said, taking a small step forward, "I would grow weaker, with the passage of time?"

She made the same gesture and again the King stumbled back. He dropped to one knee and then forced himself to stand again.

"Do you not realize, Septimus, I am no longer among the living?" She made a harsh cut in the air with her left hand, and the King screamed as he fell back.

When he got to his feet once more, Ken saw the King bled from a cut down one cheek.

Septimus howled in fear and rage, and Ken fell backward.

Anne screamed, and Brian let out a pained howl.

And Florence laughed.

"Come, Septimus, let us discuss this better."

Florence started to walk down the path towards the King.

CHAPTER 50
FEAR IS MOTIVATION

Brian threw up.

Down the front of his shirt, over the piece of wood which had pierced his shoulder from the back to the front, and he felt the sting of his flesh burned by the King.

Anne lay on the path, blood seeping from damaged eardrums.

Behind them, the flames devoured the house. Ahead of them, the King stepped back nervously, and Ken crawled forward.

Florence walked down the path towards the King.

Brian watched as the dead scattered. They ran from the scene. The street emptied quickly, and Brian saw the King drop the stuffed dog the little girl had carried with her.

Brian tried to move his right arm, but the effort caused him to scream.

He gasped for air and managed a weak, "Anne."

The sound of Ken's home as it burned drowned out Brian's voice, so he repeated her name, only louder.

She managed to look up at him. "What's happening?"

"They're fighting," Brian said. "And we need to leave."

Anne nodded and sat up. She blinked, shook her head and then she pushed herself to her feet. Brian tried to do the same but he couldn't.

Anne took him by the left arm and helped him up. Ahead of them, Brian saw Ken get to his feet and stagger towards Florence. Florence walked steadily towards the King, who retreated.

The King screamed and clapped his hands together. Trees were torn up from the road and hurled at Florence, who merely passed through them while Ken scrambled around the upturned roots.

"Septimus," Florence said, laughing, "what do you think such things would do to me? When I was flesh and blood, innocent and unwary, yes, your tricks did their damage. Even then I won out."

She snapped her fingers, and the King was thrown a dozen feet down the road.

"Perhaps not you," Septimus snarled. "What of the others?"

The King looked to Brian, made a fist and pulled his hand back violently.

Brian screamed as the wood in his shoulder was jerked out from back to front.

Florence chuckled. "What is he to me but meat? I will kill him myself when I am done, Septimus. You do nothing except save me time."

"No, Brian!" Anne said as he dropped to the ground.

He sat down, the pain intense. Anne hurried to him, shrugged her coat off and quickly pressed it on the entrance and exit points of the wound.

Ken looked back at them.

"Get out!" the old man shouted. "Get out now!"

"Can you stand up, Brian?" Anne asked.

Brian could hear the fear in her voice. She might lose what little control she had left.

"I have to," Brian said, and with Anne's help, he got to his feet once more.

CHAPTER 51
SEPTIMUS REX FORCES THE ISSUE

Ken could hardly think.

The pain was tremendous. Agony as some great device sought to break the fused seams of his skull.

"Traitor!" the King screamed. "Betrayer! I'll see you pulled apart and twisted inside out, you foul thing!"

Ken groaned, yet he continued to stumble forward with determination.

"Leave him be, Septimus," Florence snapped.

"Harlot!" Septimus shrieked. "Shut your mouth, *harlot!*"

As the last word escaped his lips, the maintenance building exploded. Debris rushed down from the night sky, and flames shot upwards. A brick struck Ken in the right shoulder and his collar bone shattered with the ease of an old branch.

Ken snarled and his rage buried the pain of his collarbone deep within itself. Suddenly an image flashed before his eyes.

Ike Fenton being thrown out of the window.

And then his friend was there.

Ike Fenton dressed as he had been the day he died, in his uniform. His friend ran to the King and slammed into him.

The scream ripped out of Septimus Rex's mouth made Ken's eyes pulse with pain, but Ken enjoyed it.

Ike landed punch after punch, until finally the King rounded on him, grasped Ike in his massive hands and tore him in half.

Ike vanished, and the King panted.

Again, Ken thought. *I must do it again.*

He pictured Clyde, and the faceless man appeared behind the King, and he held a wicked bayonet in his hands. The weapon was plunged into the King's back, and Clyde let out a cackle of pure glee.

Florence stepped forward and stamped her foot down.

The pavement rose up in a wave, rolled forward and broke upon the King.

Septimus Rex fell onto his back and screamed as the bayonet was pushed deeper into him. Clyde landed on top of him and shoved his hand into the King's mouth in an attempt to smother him.

Ken took a deep breath, and then he realized Florence was beside him.

"There is nothing to fear here, Kenneth," Florence said, looking at him. "Nothing at all. I have been there, where you're going, and returned, for I cared not for it. But you, stalwart watchman, you will ascend with the rest."

"Now," she said, looking at the King, "let us finish this beast before I cannot turn my anger away from the heathen Roy. Find yourself a piece of iron, Kenneth. Arm yourself."

Ken nodded, looked around and saw a twisted iron bar at his feet. He bent down and picked it up. With the heavy piece of metal in his hand he started to run, and Florence ran with him.

They reached the fallen King together, and with Clyde, they started to beat the unholy life from Middlebury Sanitarium's Lord and Master.

The King's screams of rage took on a higher, frenzied note of panic. He attempted to defend himself. The King locked eyes with Ken as he howled, "I made you! You are mine! I am Middlebury and Middlebury is me! You are my Watchman, set to watch over my domain!"

"Strike hard, Watchman!" Florence snarled, driving her thumbs into the King's eyes. "Listen not to the foul speech of this beast."

The King shrieked in pain and Ken struck him with all of the force he could muster.

"I am not your Watchman!" Ken screamed. "I am Middlebury's, and Middlebury is not you!"

He locked his fingers around the King's throat and choked him. He slowly squeezed the life out of the King, who writhed beneath him, his screams cut short as Florence tore his tongue out.

"I am the Watchman," Ken hissed, "and I watch over the residents of Middlebury, both the living and the dead."

The King went limp in Ken's hands and blackness crashed down upon him.

Chapter 52
Will the Morning Come?

It ended where it began.

Somehow, Brian couldn't remember exactly, he and Anne had arrived at the guardhouse. His car and Anne's were still parked at the Head Nurse's house.

She wanted to go get them, but Brian stopped her.

"We have to get outside of the gates," he said.

"Why?" she asked.

Before he could answer, a second explosion rocked the Sanitarium. In the brightly lit night sky, he saw the massive amount of debris rise up and quickly fall.

"I think this is the end," Brian said. "The end of all of it. The end of Middlebury."

He could feel himself slip into shock. He started to shake.

"Brian!" she said. "Hold on. You need a doctor."

"Yeah," he said, chuckling nervously. "But I'm pretty sure the phones will work outside of the gates. We need to get out there, Anne."

She hesitated a moment and looked at the warmth offered by the guardhouse. Then Anne shook her head, steadied him again and helped him to pass through the gates. They cleared the boundary and made their way across the road to the tree-lined edge and another explosion ripped through the air. More followed quickly, and the buildings started to collapse.

Clouds of smoke roiled out towards the guardhouse and the gates and the stonewall.

Yet the smoke seemed to strike a barrier and rose up instead of out, and curled back in upon itself. From within, the smoke shapes appeared, the shapes of people. The faint outlines of men and women and children. For the briefest of moments, the shapes stood still, and then, as one, they ascended to the heavens.

Anne looked at him, then reached out, cupped his chin in her delicate hands and held him steady as she leaned in and kissed him. The feeling was electric, her strong tongue traced the outline of his lips and she tasted incredibly sweet.

Brian pulled away, ashamed at the pleasure. He shook his head. "I can't. I can't, Anne."

"I understand," she said softly. "I just needed to know."

Jenny's face flashed before Brian's eyes and his desire to touch Anne again disappeared. Jenny was far too important, far too special to forget.

Anne was a nice girl, and pretty. But she wasn't Jenny.

"We should get you to a hospital, Brian," Anne said, and then the sound of hundreds of windows breaking cut her off.

The shattered glass fell in shards. Starlight and moonlight were reflected thousands of times. The earth shook, groaned and let out a long hiss which threatened the foundations of the world.

"Oh my God, Brian," Anne said softly. "What about Ken?"

"He must be dead, Anne," Brian said after a moment. "He must be. They all must be."

"How do you know?" she asked in a whisper. "How do you know he's dead?"

"Because Middlebury might exist without its King," Brian said, "but never without its Watchman."

Chapter 53
Back in Business

"How are you feeling?" Jenny asked, looking up from her needlepoint.

"Sore," Brian answered, bringing her a glass of red wine.

She smiled up at him, put down her stitching and took the glass. "Thanks, Babe."

"You're welcome," Brian said. He gave her a kiss on the forehead and then went to his own chair. He put his Booker's neat down on the table, picked up a book titled, *Passing Strange* about ghosts and hauntings in New England, and got comfortable.

"You made good money on Middlebury," Jenny said, looking over the edge of the wine glass at him.

"Yes," he agreed.

"And they even coughed up the money for your hospital bill," she said, raising an eyebrow.

"Well, at least I didn't have another heart attack," he said, grinning.

"Small comfort, Brian Roy," Jenny said with a sigh.

He went to speak again but the 'ghost phone' rang on the table beside Jenny. Brian closed his mouth as Jenny answered it.

"Leonidas Group, Jenny speaking."

She paused for a moment, put her wine glass down and her eyes widened. "Really? Hold on, let me tell my husband."

"What?" Brian whispered.

"Rye, New Hampshire," she said, shaking her head. "There's a headless ghost running around the Protestant Church."

Brian chuckled and looked at it his watch.

Ten minutes past six.

"Tell them I'll be there in an hour," Brian said, and Jenny shook her head as she passed on the information.

CHAPTER 54
FINDING THE WAY

When the darkness cleared, Ken found himself upright beneath the wide branches of a weeping willow tree. He could hear bird songs in the distance and the air smelled sweetly of spring.

Something rustled beside him and he turned to look.

Francine Borden stood with him. In her hands, she held her stuffed dog.

"Kenneth," she whispered. "Can you help me?"

He squatted down and looked at her. In a soft voice he asked, "What do you need help with, Francine?"

"It's time to go," she said, looking out at the canopy of whip-like branches which hung around them. "It's time to go, Kenneth, but I don't know the way. Can you help me?"

Kenneth held out his hand to her and she took it.

Her skin was warm and soft. A little girl's hand.

He smiled at her.

"Of course I can help you, Francine," he said, standing up. "We'll find the way together."

He held tightly onto her hand as she clutched her dog to her chest, and together they stepped through the veil to see what awaited them.

* * *

KEN, DECEMBER 30TH, 1969

It was three o'clock in the morning.

The sky was a stunning dark blue, the stars shining brightly and the half-moon crisp and clean.

The paths and roads in Middlebury had been shoveled by maintenance crews earlier in the day. Nearly two feet of snow had fallen the night before.

And now Ken and Ike walked in the bitter, freezing temperature. The cold bit angrily at what small amount of skin was exposed. Sand grounded loudly under their boots, and the men were wrapped up as much as they could be. Ike, somehow, had managed to convince the quartermaster of the local Army Reserve barracks to part with a couple of pairs of cold-weather goggles.

Ken and Ike wore heavy overcoats. Each designed for use in the cold. The two men walked at a pace that kept them warm and allowed them to observe the grounds.

Just because it was freezing out didn't mean Middlebury could be left to its own devices.

It always had to be watched.

"So," Ike said. "You still doing okay in Room Three?"

"What?" Ken asked. "Oh. Yeah."

"You haven't slept there at night?"

"Nope," Ken chuckled. "Keeping to the routine, like you said."

"Good. Just keep to it. Another month or two and you'll be all set with the sleep schedule. You won't have to worry about sleeping at night in the room."

Ken only nodded his agreement and tried not to think of the warmth and comfort of his bunk.

As they rounded the corner of Building Four Ike pointed ahead of them.

The lights to the house were on.

Ken had never seen them on. He had heard terrible things coming from the house. Screams, maniacal laughter, sobbing, and the painful, mournful cries of someone wracked with grief. Ken looked hard at the house and then he pointed at the chimney.

Smoke rose up from it.

Music reached Ken's ears as they moved closer to the small brick building. He strained to hear it clearly.

Schubert's 'Death and the Maiden,' Ken thought. His grandfather had loved it.

The front door to the house opened as he and Ike approached.

The music grew louder. Light burst out onto the crisp snow. Ken could smell coffee.

Ike stopped at the brick path leading to the house.

"Why are we stopping?" Ken asked.

"It's your turn," Ike said. He pointed to the house.

"What do you mean?" Ken said, looking back to the house and the open door.

"She only invites the third shift guys in," Ike said. "She decides when. Looks like tonight's your night."

Ken swallowed nervously. "I have to, huh?"

Ike nodded. "Good luck, Ken. Come back to the guardhouse as soon as she lets you out."

Ike started to walk away, and Ken said, "Hey Ike."

Ike paused and looked back.

"Anybody not come out?" Ken asked.

"A few," Ike said. "You'll be fine."

Ken watched Ike walk away and then he turned and looked at the open door.

INSIDE THE HOUSE

As Ken stepped over the threshold and into the warmth of the room, the door slammed closed behind him. His heart tried to punch its way out of his chest.

He was in a small parlor. An old, hand-cranked phonograph, with the bell-shaped speaker, turned towards him, played Schubert's symphony. Dark wood Victorian furniture stood in the room. A pair of matching chairs flanking a marble topped hearth. A small, but pleasant fire greeted Ken.

Doilies were draped over the edges of the furniture. A silver coffee service stood on a narrow tea table in the room's center.

Immediately to his left was a slim hall stand. Quietly Ken removed his winter gear, hung each piece up and finally he sat down on stand's bench to remove his boots.

A faint voice in his head whispered for him to be polite.

He needed to be on his best behavior.

With his footwear removed and placed on the rag-rug, Ken stood.

"Hello?" he asked cautiously.

A woman's voice came from an open doorway.

"Please sit down, Kenneth."

He licked his lips nervously and went and sat down in the left chair by the fire. He forced himself to put his hands palms down on his legs.

A moment later the owner of the voice came into the room on silent feet.

She looked to be in her forties and she was stunningly beautiful.

Long white hair fell well past her shoulders in thick curls. The black dress she wore accentuated her curves, and her lips were a disturbing color of red and reminded Ken of arterial blood.

Ken forced himself to remember all of his manners and he stood up as she drew closer. He gave a short bow.

"Excellent, Kenneth," she murmured. He waited until she sat down before returning to his own seat.

The volume of the symphony lowered.

"We will have coffee shortly," she said.

"Yes, Ma'am."

She smiled at him, and he saw her teeth were all filed to points. "You may call me Isabella, Kenneth."

"Thank you, Isabella."

Her smile widened. "Oh, I do like you, Kenneth. I'm ever so pleased you answered the call."

Ken frowned. "I'm sorry, Isabella. What call?"

"The call which brought you here," she said. "You see, each of you was summoned. You have all been summoned."

"To Middlebury?" Kenneth asked.

"To Middlebury," she said, nodding. "To us."

"Who are you, Isabella?" Kenneth asked.

"We are the dark things," she said pleasantly. "Those things in the shadows beneath your bed. In your closet and in your cellar. All of the terrible, haunting thoughts of your childhood."

"Oh."

She smiled. "'Oh' indeed, Kenneth."

"Why was I brought here?" Ken asked after a moment of silence.

"I wouldn't want to spoil the surprise, Kenneth," Isabella said, her voice suddenly seductive. "No, not at all."

Something thumped beneath his feet, and Ken looked down at the wood floor visible between his woolen socks.

He glanced at Isabella, and she smiled sweetly at him.

Again something struck the floor.

Ken's heart started to race.

"Go ahead, Kenneth," she said. "Go on and knock."

Ken looked at the floor once more, leaned forward and rapped on the smooth wood with his knuckles.

The response was immediate. A frenzied series of knocks accompanied by desperate screaming.

Ken sat up quickly and pressed himself into the back of his chair. He fought the urge to lift up his feet, and he looked to Isabella.

The woman steepled her long, graceful fingers together and smiled serenely at him. She sighed with pleasure. "Such a delectable sound."

Ken didn't agree, but he didn't voice his opinion either. Instead, he asked, "What is it?"

"A young man who irritated me," Isabella said, her voice growing stern. "There are several downstairs. In the cellar."

"What do they do in the cellar, Isabella?" Ken asked.

"They participate in the re-enactment of the fate of Prometheus," she said dismissively.

Ken wracked his brain for a moment and tried to remember his Greek mythology. After several long seconds, he asked, "Is there an eagle involved?"

Isabella laughed happily. "An excellent question, Kenneth. Alas, there is not. I have had to substitute a creature a trifle more mundane, and far less magnificent."

"May I ask what creature it is, Isabella?" Ken asked.

Isabella smiled playfully. "Of course, you may, Kenneth. You are proving to be an absolute delight. May I ask with whom are you paired for your duties here at Middlebury?"

"Ike," Ken answered. "Ike Fenton."

She pouted. "Hmm. Ike barely passed his interview. A well-meaning youth at the time, a trifle surly, however. He is intelligent, though, and he has lasted far longer than I had expected. So, Augustus certainly could have paired you with worse."

"I will accept your judgment on the issue of my partner, Isabella," Ken replied.

"You, Kenneth," she said, leaning forward and fairly purring, "you are truly entertaining."

Kenneth nearly jumped out of his chair as the man in the cellar pounded on the floor.

"Enough!" Isabella hissed, and the word struck Ken with the force of a fist. "I'm so sorry, Kenneth. Please, forgive me, I became distracted."

"No need for apologies, Isabella," Ken managed to say.

She smiled at him, her tongue flicking out across sharpened teeth. "Now, you were curious as to what animal has replaced the kingly eagle?"

Kenneth could only nod.

"Rats," Isabella said. "Rats."

"A rat per man?" Ken asked.

She chuckled and shook her head. "No. Not at all, Kenneth. Rats. Multiple rats for all of them. If you like, I could take you downstairs?"

"No thank you, Isabella," Ken said, forcing a smile. "I don't know as I have the stomach for such a sight."

"No? I suppose not," she sighed. "Although I must confess I do gain some small amount of satisfaction when I watch the rats burrow into them."

Someone screamed, and Ken gripped the arms of the chair tightly.

"I remember when you saw worse," Isabella said in a sly voice. "Oh yes. We all do."

Ken looked at her.

"We were there, you know," Isabella continued. "In the rice paddies, filthy with human waste as you tried to save those men, dragging them to your flying machine. Oh yes, Kenneth. We were there."

He looked at her, unsure of how to respond.

"And do you remember, the body you found as a boy? The one tucked under the bridge and ready to pop? Swollen in the summer's heat?"

Ken tried to answer but he couldn't. His mouth was too dry, and his throat nearly closed with fear.

"One never forgets the smell of death, Kenneth," she whispered. "I remember my first smell of it. Here, at this place. My doctor in Boston believed the New Hampshire air would do my frail constitution good. I came here. To the Middlebury Sanitarium. So many of us with tuberculosis, Kenneth."

Isabella stood up and moved to the tea table. She poured coffee into two cups and carried one to Ken.

"Thank you," Ken whispered.

She smiled and returned to her chair.

He took a cautious sip and found the coffee strong and bitter, the way he preferred it. She took a drink of her own, and then she continued to speak.

"You could smell the sickness in the air," Isabella said. "You could literally taste death, Kenneth. The disease added a tang to it, you know. It created a flavor nearly irresistible. With every bite, you wanted more."

Ken took another drink of coffee, returned the cup to the saucer and asked slowly, "Every bite?"

"Indeed," she said. "Tuberculosis settles into the very marrow of the bones, but only in the lungs does one find the truly heady spice of the sickness."

She smiled, revealing once more the sharp teeth behind her sensual lips.

"You filed your teeth," Ken said, "so you could eat better."

"You, Kenneth, are only the second person in half a century who made the connection," she said, laughing happily. "Do you know who the first was?"

Ken could only shake his head as he tried not to think about the beautiful woman before him living as a cannibal.

"Augustus," Isabella sighed. She smiled at him. "Now finish your coffee, Kenneth. I've something to show you."

Looking at Middlebury Sanitarium

Ken felt naked without his boots.

He was certain he would only survive by doing what she wanted, and by being as polite as possible.

The occasional thump from the cellar reminded him of the others who had failed.

Isabella did not walk in front of him. She glided. She held her hands genteelly in front of her as she moved silently along the hardwood floor. She led him through the parlor, down a short hall and into a room on the left which was disturbingly large.

This place is too big, Ken thought, looking around at the windowless walls.

Isabella glanced at him slyly, a smirk on her face.

"You see the trick?" she asked.

"The room, Isabella?" Ken said. "How can it be this size?"

"I have been here an extremely long time, Kenneth," she answered. "The house does what I want it to. Look at the table."

Ken turned his attention to the center of the room. A long table lay hidden beneath a white sheet. Isabella gestured nonchalantly with her hand, and the sheet rose up, slid off to the far side and collapsed onto the floor.

Ken stifled a gasp.

A model of Middlebury Sanitarium stretched out before him. It was done in exquisite detail. All of the houses, the paths, the trees. Everything looking as though it had been plucked from reality and merely shrunk to fit the miniature.

"This is his domain," Isabella said softly. "Where he reigns supreme."

"Who does, Isabella?" Ken asked.

She turned and looked at him. Something dark and frightening passed across her face, and she smiled. The vicious teeth parted ever so slightly.

"Septimus Rex."

Ken couldn't hide his confusion.

"Worry not, young Kenneth," Isabella said. "He will have you pay your tribute in time. For now, however, you are mine."

Ken took an involuntary step back. A vision of her teeth sinking into his flesh set his hands to trembling.

"So you know fear?" she asked mockingly.

"Of course, I do, Isabella," Ken managed to say. "Why wouldn't I?"

"A brave man can admit his fear. But," she said with a sigh, "I digress. Look upon the Sanitarium, Kenneth."

Ken turned his attention back to the model.

"This small building here, do you see it?" she asked, pointing at a small house tucked off to the left. He knew it, of course. He passed it each night on his rounds.

"Yes, Isabella, I see it."

"The house is yours," she said. "It is where you will live."

"But I live in a dormitory," Ken said, confused, "and the head janitor for Building Two lives there."

"You're using the wrong tense, Kenneth," Isabella smiled.

"I'm sorry, what do you mean, Isabella?"

"He lived there, Kenneth," she said in an easy tone. "Lived there."

"Oh."

She smiled again and flashed her sharpened teeth. She gestured with her hand, and the sheet rose up to cover the model. "Come now, Kenneth, let us retire to the parlor for one more cup of coffee. I am sure Ike is becoming quite worried about you."

Ken didn't say anything as he followed her back to the parlor. She motioned for him to sit as she filled the coffee cups. As he accepted his cup, Ken noticed a covered plate on the table beside the silver service.

"My dinner," she smiled wickedly. "Would you care for a taste, Kenneth?"

"No thank you, Isabella."

The food did smell delightful, though. It had a smoky scent, as though it had just been taken off of a grill. He smelled potatoes as well, and gravy. His mouth started to water, and he forced himself to focus on the coffee. Once he finished the drink, he set the cup down on the tray and looked to Isabella, who watched him with interest.

"You enjoy the smell, don't you," she said in a low voice, clearly interested.

"Yes, Isabella," he answered.

"How curious. How curious." She set her coffee down and stood up. "I shall help you get dressed, Kenneth. Then you will go away, of course, and set your friend's mind at ease."

"Yes, Isabella," Ken said.

"Perhaps you can visit again?" she asked.

"Will I be allowed to?" Ken asked in return.

She laughed. "If the door is open, then you may come in, Kenneth. Otherwise, I may be indisposed."

Ken smiled, bent down and pulled on his boots, lacing them up quickly. Isabella helped him with his coat and hat, his scarf and mittens.

"There," she said with a nod, taking a step back. "You look prepared for hell, Kenneth."

"Thank you, Isabella," he said, giving a short bow. He could feel the sweat already starting as she walked back to her chair and sat down.

He turned, grasped the doorknob and looked back at her. Isabella lifted the cover off of her dinner and revealed the repast.

A pair of black almost charred pieces of meat were artfully arranged upon a bed of potatoes. The smell was agonizingly delicious.

"Do you know what the smell is, Kenneth?" Isabella asked.

Ken shook his head.

"Fifty-eight years of smoking hand-rolled cigarettes," she said pleasantly. "The janitor, he started when he was thirteen. His lungs will be absolutely exquisite."

TALKING ABOUT THE NIGHT

Ken hurried along the path to the guardhouse. The air was a little warmer, and he found himself sweating by the time he reached the building.

Ike was there with a rosary in his hands.

"Ken?!" Ike said, jumping up out of his chair. He wrapped his arms around Ken and gave him a huge hug. "Damn, boy!"

Ken laughed and collapsed into the chair as Ike closed the door and turned around to face him.

"I didn't think you were coming back," Ike said, stuffing the rosary beads into a breast pocket. "None of us did."

"Why?" Ken asked, confused. "How long was I gone?"

"Five days," Ike said.

Ken blinked. "What?"

"Five days," Ike repeated. "And there was so much noise coming from the house we had to divert traffic around it. The screams we heard. I was scared, Ken. I won't lie. We tried to get in but every time we opened the door the screaming would stop, and the house was empty. Top to bottom."

"Jesus," Ken whispered.

Ike nodded. "Yeah. Doing a lot of praying for you, kid. Hold on, though, I've got to call Gus."

Ken moved to one side as Ike reached over, took the phone off of the receiver and dialed Gus' number.

"Hello Anna," Ike said, "It's Ike over at Middlebury. Yes. Yes, it's important. Please tell him Ken's back."

Ike held the phone to his ear and then a moment later Ken heard Gus' voice, "Ike, he's back?!"

"Yup, right here in the guardhouse with me, Gus."

"Put him on, Ike. Put him on."

Ike handed Ken the phone, and he took it. He pulled off his hat and put the phone to his ear. "Hi, Gus."

"Ken!" Gus said happily. "My God, boy, we were worried sick about you."

"I'm sorry," Ken said, "it didn't feel more than an hour."

"No, no, I'm not mad at you or anything," Gus said. "Now listen, you stay in the guardhouse with Ike. I don't want you going out to patrol at all. Besides, your shift is almost done. Another two hours. You wait for me there. Understand?"

"Yes," Ken said.

"Good. Put Ike back on, please," Gus said.

Ken handed the phone back to Ike.

Ike took it. "What do you need me to do, Gus? Yes. Yes, of course. Right. Okay, we'll see you at seven, Gus. Be safe."

Ike hung up the phone, leaned up against the wall and looked at Ken. "You met her?"

"Isabella?" Ken asked.

Ike nodded.

"Yeah. Yeah, I met her." Ken paused and then he said, "Did you speak with her when you went in?"

Ike's eyes widened, and he shook his head. "Hell no. I... I went in, and she was standing there, in the dark. No light except for what was coming in through the window. Full moon, you know?"

Ken nodded.

"Well, anyway, I stood there for a few minutes, just staring at her, and then she smiled, Ken. She smiled and those teeth!" Ike closed his eyes, took a deep breath and then he continued, "Anyway, after she smiled I said something. I don't remember what. Sort of like a dream. I knew I was speaking, I just didn't know what I was saying. But she laughed, and the door opened. I took off out of there."

"Did you hear anything?" Ken asked. "Other than her, I mean."

Ike frowned, and he shook his head. "No. Not a thing. You did?"

"Yeah," Ken said.

"Don't tell me," Ike said in a low voice, glancing out the front window and into the dark. "Let's wait 'til Gus gets here. I don't want to hear it more than once."

Ken nodded.

He didn't want to tell it more than once.

They sat in a comfortable silence and listened to the small wall clock ticking off the minutes. The radio squawked occasionally when a team checked in, and several times the teams came through. They crowded in to warm up, congratulate Ken on his return, and then continued on their way.

Less than an hour later, Gus arrived. He called Sean McGuire in to watch the front and brought Ken and Ike across the road to his small office in Building One. Gus turned all the lights on, opened up the floor vent to let the heat in fully, and took a bottle of rye whiskey out of his desk. He took off the cap, had a pull from the bottle and passed it on to Ike. Ike did the same before he handed it to Ken.

Ken happily had a drink. He winced at the burning sensation the whiskey created as it blazed down his throat, but it was worth it. With a grin, he handed the bottle back to Gus. The older man left it open and on his desk.

"Sit down, gentlemen, sit down," Gus said, sitting in his own seat behind the desk. Once they had gotten comfortable, Gus leaned forward and said, "Alright, Ken. Let's hear it. Every last detail."

Ken started to talk. He told them everything, from the moment he entered to when he stepped back into the cold.

"Claude Lozeau died yesterday," Gus said when Ken had finished. "He was the janitor. They put him in the incinerator at the crematorium. He didn't have any family. Plus, the morgue's just about filled up."

"You think they were his lungs?" Ike asked.

Gus nodded. "You know, Ike. I've never heard of her speaking to someone for so long. She say anything as to why?"

"No," Ken said. "She mentioned you. She mentioned Ike. Talked about the ones underneath the house. Someone named Septimus Rex."

And Ken stopped.

Gus had straightened up. The color drained from his face. His hand shook violently as he reached out, picked up the bottle of whiskey and took a long, deep drink. His cheeks were flushed as he put the bottle back on the table.

He cleared his throat and then he asked, "She said 'Septimus Rex?'"

Ken nodded.

"And she told you they want you in Claude's place?" he asked.

"Yeah," Ken said.

"Get home. Start packing. We'll have you into Claude's place by the early afternoon the latest," Gus said. He turned his attention to Ike. "Ike, I want all of the third shift guys to meet with me when they punch out. Includes you, too."

"And me?" Ken asked as he and Ike stood up.

Gus shook his head, took another drink and said, "No. You'll be fine. The rest of these boys... well, maybe not."

Ken watched as Gus turned to look out the office window. Beyond the glass, the sky was brighter. The air disturbingly clear.

It would be cold again.

"Come on, kid," Ike said, gently taking Ken by the arm, "we've got things to do."

Ken nodded, and they left Gus in his chair, the whiskey bottle cradled in his hands.

MOVING INTO CLAUDE'S HOUSE

Claude's house wasn't ready in the afternoon.

Ken had spent all day packing up his few belongings, washing his clothes, and getting his room cleaned. The army had taught him how to clean, and how to keep things clean.

When he was done in his room, the floors were spotless. He had removed the cap to the shower's drain and cleaned out what he found. He had even cleaned up and under the sink, just the way the Drill Sergeants in basic training had showed him.

At four thirty in the afternoon, he sat on his stripped mattress, his few belongings stacked against the far wall.

A knock sounded at his door.

"Come in," Ken said tiredly.

The door open and Gus walked in. "How are you doing, kid?"

"Tired."

Gus nodded. "Understood. Now listen, Claude's place isn't ready just yet. Should be done soon. Probably after chow."

"Okay," Ken said. "Sounds good."

"Ike or Sean will swing by when the house is set, load up your stuff in a maintenance truck and get you squared away. I've already got Leonard from the kitchen putting a box of dry goods together for you. You'll have some stuff to hold you over until you can get into town and pick up some grub."

"Thanks, Gus," Ken said. "I appreciate it."

Gus smiled. "Now listen, don't go to sleep, okay?"

Ken frowned at him. "Why not?"

"Well, you've been sleeping during the day, right?" Gus asked.

"Yeah," Ken answered.

"You've been safe. Mary doesn't seem to mind people sleeping during the day. Just not at night. So don't fall asleep. She won't like it."

"What'll happen?" Ken asked

"Just don't, fall asleep," Gus said, the smile dropped away. "You start to sleep, you stand up. Okay?"

"Sure," Ken said. "Sure."

"Alright," Gus said, looking at him with concern. "I've got to go. My wife needs to get up to see her sister and I'm driving. I'll try and send one of the boys over on my way out."

"Okay, Gus," Ken said. "Safe home."

Gus paused at the door for a moment, as though he had another thing to add, but then he shook his head and left.

As he sat on the bed, Ken realized the dining facility wouldn't open for dinner for another thirty minutes.

And Ken was tired. So tired. He hadn't slept since the day before, perhaps longer.

At the thought of sleep, he yawned.

I'm forgetting something. Something someone told me.

He yawned again.

The mattress was soft beneath him, and he fought the urge to stretch out on it. He tried to make himself stand, but he couldn't.

He was too tired.

Ken closed his eyes and focused on being awake.

He felt as though he was floating in the air.

Everything was calm and peaceful.

"Why are you special?" a woman asked.

"I don't know," Ken said with a sigh.

"Why wasn't I?"

"Don't know," he said, trying to roll over.

"Why wasn't I?!" she shrieked, and the door slammed shut.

The lightbulb in the wall sconce popped, and the temperature in the room plummeted.

Ken tried to stand and found he couldn't.

Something suspended him above the bed. Above the floor.

And then it spun him around and slammed him into a wall. He groaned as he struck the cement. The air rushed out of him as he struck the cold tile of the floor and he gasped as he struggled to gain his feet.

Blows rained down upon his head and neck. Small hands delivering brutally powerful and cold punches.

Ken managed to get to his hands and knees before a foot kicked him in the groin from behind. He dry heaved as he fell back to the floor. He clutched at his privates and tried to roll into a ball.

"Why are you so special?!" the woman screamed. "Tell me why!!"

The punches and kicks were furious, the power in each matched the rage in her voice.

Ken coughed and tasted blood, the iron tang foul on his tongue.

"Enough!" he yelled.

And the thing stopped.

"Who are you?" she hissed.

"Leave me alone," Ken said, rolling onto his side and coughing.

"Tell me your name," she demanded.

Ken sat up. "Kenneth Buckingham. What's yours?"

"It is not," she whispered.

"I think I know my own name," Ken said angrily.

"It is not!" she screamed, and she attacked him again. The violence of her blows grew in intensity. Ken felt his eyes roll up, and his breathing became shallow. He twisted on the floor and saw a slim line of light.

The door.

He started to crawl towards it.

"No!" she shrieked, grabbing him by a foot and dragging him back.

The door flew open and light burst into the room. Ken winced at the sudden brightness.

"Jesus!" Ike shouted.

Ken heard the heavy 'chock' sound of a round being chambered into a shotgun quickly followed by a flash of light and a simultaneous, thunderous roar.

The woman howled and still tried to drag Ken backward.

Ike fired the shotgun twice more and something burned into Ken's calves even as the unseen woman dropped his foot.

A flashlight came on, and the bright beam lit up the room.

"Christ on a crutch, Ken," Ike said. "Are you alive?"

"Yeah," Ken said hoarsely. "Yeah."

"Well, guess the first stop's the infirmary for you. Get those cuts treated and the rock salt out of your legs."

"What?" Ken asked, groaning as Ike laid the shotgun on the floor and helped him to sit up. "Rock salt?"

"Only stuff that'll scare a ghost away. Even then, when it's someone like Mary it's going to take more than one or two shots," Ike said. He sighed and pulled Ken to his feet. "Claude's place is ready."

"Oh," Ken said tightly, trying to ignore the pain. "That's good."

"Yup," Ike said, guiding Ken into the hall. "Hell, son, looks like Joe Lewis worked you over for a bit."

"Feels like it," Ken grunted.

"Well, what did I tell you?"

"About what?" Ken asked as they stopped long enough for Ike to pull open the exit door.

"I told you not to fall asleep in three, kid," Ike said with a sigh as he opened the door. "Mary, well, she ain't overly fond of men."

"Guess not," Ken said as they stepped out into the cold.

"Nope," Ike agreed. Ken winced as Ike got him down the stairs and into a maintenance truck. A moment later, Ike climbed into the driver's seat and put the truck in gear. Ike looked over at the dorm and shook his head.

"What?" Ken asked, looking.

Ike pointed at the window to Room Three.

As Ken looked, someone, ripped the shade out of the window.

"You really upset her, Ken," Ike said. "Let's just hope she doesn't follow you home."

Ken twisted around in the seat to look at the room, and he jumped as the window exploded outward from the building. The shotgun landed in the snow.

Oh, Jesus, Ken thought, turning away and closing his eyes.

* * *

Check out these best-selling series from our talented authors:

GHOST STORIES

RON RIPLEY
BERKLEY STREET SERIES
MOVING IN SERIES
HAUNTED COLLECTION SERIES
DEATH HUNTER SERIES

IAN FORTEY
JIGSAW OF SOULS SERIES
CULT OF THE ENDLESS NIGHT SERIES

SUPERNATURAL SUSPENSE

A. I. NASSER
SLAUGHTER SERIES
SIN SERIES

DAVID LONGHORN
NIGHTMARE SERIES
ASYLUM SERIES

SARA CLANCY
THE BELL WITCH SERIES
BANSHEE SERIES

For a complete list of our new releases and best-selling horror books, visit
ScareStreet.com or scan the QR code below!